DUST

ALSO BY DUSTI BOWLING

Across the Desert

The Canyon's Edge

DUST

DUSTI BOWLING

LITTLE, BROWN AND COMPANY
New York   Boston

Copyright © 2023 by Dusti Bowling
Illustrations copyright © 2023 by Yaoyao Ma Van As
Discussion guide copyright © 2023 by
Little, Brown and Company

Cover art copyright © 2023 by Yaoyao Ma Van As
Cover design by Karina Granda
Cover copyright © 2023 by Hachette Book Group, Inc.
Interior design by Carla Weise

Little, Brown and Company
Hachette Book Group
1290 Avenue of the Americas, New York, NY 10104
Visit us at LBYR.com

First Edition: August 2023

Little, Brown and Company is a division of Hachette Book Group, Inc.
The Little, Brown name and logo are trademarks of
Hachette Book Group, Inc.

The publisher is not responsible for websites (or their content) that are not owned by the publisher.

Little, Brown books may be purchased in bulk for business, educational, or promotional use. For information, please contact your local bookseller or the Hachette Book Group Special Markets Department at special.markets@hbgusa.com.

Library of Congress Cataloging-in-Publication Data
Names: Bowling, Dusti, author.
Title: Dust : a novel / by Dusti Bowling.
Description: First edition. | New York : Little, Brown and Company, 2023. | Audience: Ages 10–14. | Summary: When a boy with a terrible secret moves to town, there is a sudden increase in dust storms, and asthmatic Avalyn theorizes the storms are linked to his emotions and tries to help as she struggles to breathe.
Identifiers: LCCN 2022033954 | ISBN 9780316414234 (hardcover) | ISBN 9780316414357 (ebook)
Subjects: CYAC: Friendship—Fiction. | Bullies and bullying—Fiction. | Asthma—Fiction. | Dust—Fiction. | LCGFT: Novels.
Classification: LCC PZ7.1.B6872 Du 2023 | DDC [Fic]—dc23
LC record available at https://lccn.loc.gov/2022033954

ISBNs: 978-0-316-41423-4 (hardcover), 978-0-316-41435-7 (ebook)

Printed in the United States of America

LSC-C

Printing 1, 2023

For the child who needs it.

You *can* speak out.

You *can* say stop.

You *can* fight back.

DUST

Prologue.
P-R-O-L-O-G-U-E.
Prologue.

I was a toddler the first time I almost died. We were living in Oklahoma, and the air was so humid, we could barely see our neighbor's house. At least that's what my parents tell me. I don't remember because I was only two.

Humidity that thick is like steam rising off a bubbling witch's brew made of several ingredients: mold, pollen, ragweed, smoke, and dust. Pollution stew. It all hangs suspended in the heavy air, making my airways tighten so that I cough because I feel like I'm breathing air mud. Or sky slime. Or spaghetti sauce. Basically imagine trying to breathe sludge, and that's how I feel during an asthma attack. Then throw a big boulder on your chest and shove a stone down your throat.

I was having a hard time breathing that day ten years ago, so Mom gave me an extra treatment while Dad was at work. She kept my inhaler in her pocket, where one has been ever since. She hadn't showered in days, afraid of leaving my side for even five minutes, but I seemed to be doing all right after using the nebulizer. I was giggling at Elmo on TV. She didn't hear any wheezing, so she went to wash off three days of worry and sweat and anxiety.

It only takes a few minutes for a person to suffocate.

When Mom came out, hair still dripping wet, a towel wrapped around her middle, she thought I was asleep. But my fingernails were blue, and she couldn't get me to wake up.

She called 911, then picked me up and sprayed my inhaler into my mouth, but it can't get into your lungs when your whole airway is swollen shut. Then she did mouth-to-mouth until the paramedics showed up.

I spent three days in the hospital recovering from that asthma attack.

Mom and Dad decided we had to leave Oklahoma after that. They asked the doctors where we should go. They wanted to know where I could breathe the best. The doctors told them a lot of people take their kids to Arizona, where it's dry, the allergens are low, and freezing winds don't blow. Of course, the one downside of the desert is dust, so my parents chose the least windy place they could find—Clear Canyon City, a town surrounded by mountains that block the wind, making the air still and clear.

My parents have always told me that every breath I take is precious because I so easily could have stopped breathing at two years old. Breath is important, maybe the most important thing in the world. We can't live without it for more than a few minutes. Breath is powerful. We can't speak without it. My parents also tell me that what I choose to do with my breath can change the world. What will I do with all these breaths I may not have had?

Well, I've been able to breathe pretty well for the last ten years, though I can't say I've done anything super important with those breaths—mostly a lot of talking with my two best friends and spelling every spelling bee word in existence and bickering with my parents about my room being a "pigsty."

It's amazing how little we think about our

breath when it comes easily. Of course, I still have to use my inhaler and sometimes even do a breathing treatment when the wind becomes too intense for the mountains to block and the dust swirls. But it's been manageable.

Until now.

Until Adam came to Clear Canyon City with his downcast eyes and quiet voice and horrible dark secrets.

And the dust.

It was like he brought the dust with him. And now all I can think about is breath.

chapter 1

Portentous.
P-O-R-T-E-N-T-O-U-S.
Portentous.

On Saturday morning at 9:32, all three of our phones screeched the warning at the same time. I wasn't allowed to have my phone at the kitchen table, so it was shrieking on the counter nearby. Mom and Dad picked theirs up because *they* were apparently allowed to have phones at the kitchen table. Parents could be hypocritical like that. Or as Dad would say, *As supreme ruler of the universe, I'm allowed to do what I want.*

Mom dropped her forkful of buckwheat pancake,

her face filled with both surprise and confusion. "Dust storm?"

"In Phoenix?" I asked.

Dad slowly shook his head, studying his own phone, his eyebrows drawn together. "It says Clear Canyon City."

The three of us all looked at one another before jumping out of our chairs and hurrying to the kitchen window, hands and noses pressed against the glass, searching for the dust. The air was growing hazy, which *was* sort of strange for this time of year. It definitely got a little dusty around here every now and then, especially when the big monsoon storms hit, but this time of year was usually nice and clear.

I turned to Dad, who had his lips pursed and eyes squinted. Individual strands of his gray-speckled brown hair were beginning to rise and stand up. Lifting my hand from the glass, I pointed at his head. "Whoa. Your hair." Then I saw that Mom's longer blond strands were starting to hover as well. I touched a finger to her bare freckled arm, and a spark of electricity shocked both of us. I yelped and snatched my hand away.

"Ouch!" She rubbed her arm and shot me an accusing look, as though I'd deliberately attacked her with electrical powers. Then Dad reached over and touched my arm, zapping me again, and we all burst into a sort of nervous laughter.

"What in the world?" Mom said as she and Dad rushed out the front door to see what else they could see. "Avalyn, get your butt back in that house," Mom ordered when she saw me following them. Yeah, she could be pretty bossy. If Dad was the supreme ruler, then she was the *supremer* ruler. I probably should've listened, though. To say that dust was hard on my lungs would be an understatement. It didn't help that we'd had almost no rain in a year. The desert dirt had become as fine and dry as the powdered sugar sprinkled over my buckwheat pancakes that morning.

The three of us stood side by side in our front yard, mouths open, gaping at the wall of light brown. It was like a gigantic, muddy, frothy wave crashing toward us in slow motion. Mom reached into her pocket and pulled out the inhaler she always carried, even when I wasn't with her. I guess it probably made her feel better—like as long as she carried it, I would always be safe no matter what. Dad carried one, too.

Mom passed me the inhaler, and when her hand brushed mine, it was as though her wonder, confusion, and fear seeped out of her skin and got absorbed into mine, entering my bloodstream and flowing through my body, making my veins vibrate.

"You should go back inside, Avalyn," she mumbled, sort of dreamily.

I didn't move.

"We need to make sure all the windows are closed," Dad added, as hypnotized as Mom.

The massive brown cloud erased everything in its path, completely enveloping the mountains that normally blocked the wind and kept us safe from the worst of the storms. Our hills were nothing more than speed bumps in its way.

I'd only seen dust storms like this online—big, dirty woolly blankets that slowly unrolled over the flat valley of Phoenix, shrouding homes and skyscrapers and cars in a dense darkness even headlights couldn't cut through, bringing the whole city to a pause, dramatic news anchors declaring that residents needed to take cover from the coming haboob. Everyone loved using that word. At least in my house. We'd always had a good laugh about it.

But as I stared at the relentless wall closing in on us with every breath, blocking out the light and turning day to night, I didn't feel so much like laughing, especially as my chest began to ache and tighten.

This wasn't normal. This wasn't natural. Arizona dust storms didn't behave this way.

Like finding shapes in the white clouds high in the sky, I could find shapes in this brown cloud low to the earth. The shapes puffed and swirled and formed into letters in my head. I spelled so much that my brain had started finding letters in everything—the noodles on my plate, the rocks on the desert floor, the smears on the car window. And even in this terrifying cloud.

P-E-R-I-L-O-U-S.

O-M-I-N-O-U-S.

P-O-R-T-E-N-T-O-U-S.

Something was coming.

And it wasn't just dust.

chapter 2

Anomaly.
A-N-O-M-A-L-Y.
Anomaly.

I first saw Adam on Monday in social studies. The dust storm on Saturday hadn't lasted long, but since then, it was like some kind of haze had been building in the air. The world outside the windows looked sun-bleached and washed out.

Mr. Cumberland, my social studies teacher, was droning on about the Renaissance, and I was counting down until class ended, my eyes darting from the digital clock on the wall to the windows, then back to the clock—forty-two minutes left. I was so stinking bored; my only real interest in the Renaissance was spelling it.

Renaissance. R-E-N-A-I-S-S-A-N-C-E. Renaissance.

Language: French.

Meaning: re (back, again) + naissance (birth) = rebirth.

As long as I knew the language of origin and the meaning of a word, I could usually figure out the spelling, even if I'd never heard it before. Words were puzzles like that. Fun puzzles.

Thirty-nine minutes were left in class when a boy walked in. We turned our heads.

He wore all black: black sweats, black T-shirt, black boots. His clothes made his pale skin pop, as white as the dry-erase board with *The Renaissance Period* scrawled across the top in Mr. Cumberland's messy handwriting.

The boy stared down at the thin blue carpet, his greasy, overgrown, dark brown hair hiding his face. Mr. Cumberland stopped speaking. The boy raised the crumpled paper in his hand without lifting his head, and Mr. Cumberland took it from him, reading it quickly.

In a roomful of thirty students, for some reason

the boy glanced up and looked directly at me, just for a split second, before looking back down. I hadn't been doing anything but sitting there as quietly as possible, so I had no idea why I'd caught his attention.

Mr. Cumberland shoved the note into his pocket. "Everyone, this is Adam. He's going to be with us for the remainder of the year."

Still Adam didn't look up or say anything, and neither did anyone else, though I did hear a few whispers and then snorts.

Finally, Mr. Cumberland spoke again. "You can take that seat back there in the corner." He waved his hand toward an empty seat, and Adam hurried to it. On his way to the back of the room, Adam stumbled and accidentally bumped me. When he touched me, I gasped.

My brain flashed back to the blow-up play pool Dad bought me when I was little. Every day the pool had sagged and let a little water out, and Dad had to refill both the air and water. Then one morning I raced outside, pink pool noodle in one hand, squirt gun in the other, but the pool was flat, all the water having soaked into the hot desert dirt. The pool had a rip, and it had finally grown too big to fix.

I'd often felt as though I had a rip in my chest, and drops of my insides would seep out like the air and water trickling out of my blow-up play pool. But this feeling was different from anything I'd ever felt before. It was as though air had somehow poured *into* the rip.

Way too much air.

The pool popped from the pressure, the water bursting out in a big explosive gush. I felt like *all* my insides had poured out, puddling on my desk and dribbling onto the floor, leaving me as flat, empty, and useless as my beloved pool. Leaving me with an overwhelming sense of loneliness.

I tried to cover my gasp with a cough and sank down in my seat, wishing I could stuff myself back inside through the rip. Mr. Cumberland continued with whatever he'd been talking about before Adam got here, but I couldn't focus on social studies.

Sometimes it seemed like I could feel what other people were feeling, as though I absorbed their emotions. It made me feel like Empath from X-Men.

Empath and I had some similarities, but we weren't exactly the same. First of all, Empath was super evil. Also, he could control people's emotions, and as far as I could tell, I could only sense them. But still, I couldn't find anyone else online who had the same ability, and so I'd never told anyone about it, not even Mom and Dad. I seemed to be some kind of anomaly.

Anomaly. A-N-O-M-A-L-Y. Anomaly.

I sank down further in my seat, the hollowness echoing inside my chest, my insides taking far too long to fill back up. My anxiety turned into a twist tie, squeezing my hollow balloon of a body, cutting off my circulation and air. My pulse sped up, stomach gurgled, skin flushed. Somehow all that empty space made it harder to breathe. I pulled out my inhaler and took a loud puff in the silent room.

Bryden's head darted in my direction. He wrapped his hands around his neck and mimicked gasping and choking, while the kids around him hid their smirks.

My face heated. I pressed my cool, shaking palms to my burning cheeks, hoping no one noticed how red they probably were.

I wished right then that I was exactly like Empath. I'd make Bryden feel disgusted with himself for acting like that. I'd make him feel like he'd just let out a fart that made the classroom walls rattle. But I didn't have that power, no matter how hard I'd tried in the past. And, believe me, I *had* tried. Instead, I imagined Bryden's gasps and chokes turning into letters that flew across the classroom in my direction.

L lashed me.

A abused me.

M marred me.

B bruised me.

A assaulted me.

S struck me.

T thrashed me.

E echoed in my head.

Lambaste. L-A-M-B-A-S-T-E. Lambaste.

They could make fun of my asthma and my friends and anything else they wanted, but my spelling was something I would never let them ruin again. Maybe that was part of why I loved it so much. It was just for me. They wouldn't even know I was doing it until the spelling bee. And I was better at it than all of them, which they'd find out soon enough.

Bryden lost interest in me and turned his attention toward Adam. "Nice hair. Ever heard of a shower?"

Adam's head was lowered on his thin, pale arms. I

couldn't see his face or any sign that he'd even heard Bryden.

Mr. Cumberland cleared his throat. "That is *not* how we greet new students, Bryden. I don't want to hear that from you again. Understand?"

Bryden shrugged. "Whatever."

When the bell finally rang thirty-seven agonizing minutes later, Adam lifted his head from his arms for the first time and hurried out of class. I jumped from my seat and followed him outside, scanning the whole area, shielding my eyes from the sun, but he was nowhere in sight.

Where had he come from? Why did he come here? Why was he starting at a new school in the middle of the year?

And what was that feeling I'd gotten from him?

I stood outside long enough for my lungs to start rebelling against the strange new haze in the air. I had to take another puff of my inhaler before hurrying to my next class.

chapter 3

Unconventional.
U-N-C-O-N-V-E-N-T-I-O-N-A-L.
Unconventional.

The haze seemed to have mostly cleared up the next morning, so my parents let me walk to school. They actually encouraged me to walk whenever I could because my lungs need the exercise. Plus I lived only about a mile away, so it was quicker than riding the bus.

I wandered down the road, taking my time, not in any rush to get to class, grateful the weather was still cool this early in the morning. The hedgehog cactuses were starting to bloom, and I stopped to take a picture of the pretty pink flowers with my phone. A couple of quail ran through the desert. Even though I knew it was probably still too early in the year, I kept my phone camera ready in case there were any trailing babies.

I'd probably had my own phone a lot longer than most kids. Mom and Dad installed a bunch of stuff on it, including a breathing log, emergency medical and medication instructions, and an app called Family Tracker, which told them exactly where I was at all times in case I had a severe asthma attack and couldn't call for help or explain where I was located. Dad named my phone Big Brother since it was always watching over me.

I spotted someone walking ahead of me—a dark figure, all black clothes. It looked like that new kid from my social studies class. As I neared him, Adam glanced back, saw me, then turned and picked up speed, disappearing around a corner. I turned the corner after him, but I still didn't see him anywhere.

Suddenly he leaped out from behind a big saguaro. "Why are you following me?"

My heart jumped, and I froze in place, my breath catching in my throat.

He stared at me, waiting for an answer.

I had to force myself to breathe again. "You scared me," I wheezed, pulling out my inhaler and taking a puff.

"Well? Why are you chasing me?"

I held my breath for a few seconds, making sure the medicine got deep into my lungs, before answering him. "I wasn't chasing you. I live down here. I'm going to school. It has nothing to do with you."

He whipped around and started walking away. Despite already feeling breathless, I hurried to catch up with him. "Do you live near here, too?"

"I guess," he muttered.

I stopped again and hunched over, putting my hands on my thighs for support, the inhaler slipping from my fingers onto the ground. I focused on slowing my breaths. I wanted to talk to Adam, but how could I talk when I couldn't breathe?

Adam glanced back. I expected he would keep going, but he stopped. "What's wrong with you?"

"I have asthma. Running's hard on my lungs." I forced a smile. "See? So I can't be chasing you. Unless it's a very slow chase."

He picked up the inhaler at my feet. "Are you okay?"

I nodded. "I just need a sec."

I reached for my inhaler, and he handed it to me, his fingers brushing mine. Again, I felt the air trying to fill me up to bursting, but there was something else in his touch today. It was like how my mom felt when I was sick and she slept next to me, one arm draped over my stomach to feel my breathing throughout the night. It always filled my chest with a warmth that ached, but not necessarily in a bad way.

It was concern. Genuine concern. He was worried about me. He wasn't like Bryden. He wasn't like any of the Meanie Butt Band. I stood up and faced him.

His scowl had softened, and he chewed on his lip. "I heard you use that thing in social studies."

"It's my inhaler," I explained. "Albuterol? It opens my lungs."

"Do you need it a lot?"

"Not usually. Just the last few days since it's been a little hazy."

"Are you okay, then?"

I nodded, my gaze falling to his middle, where I realized he had a comic book gripped under his arm. I pointed at it. "Oh, you like X-Men?"

He shrugged.

"I like X-Men," I said.

He tilted his head. "Really?"

"Yes, really."

"Who's your favorite character?"

I felt totally put on the spot, so I said the first name that came to mind. "Magneto."

He snorted. "How predictable."

"Well...maybe Empath."

His eyes brightened, as though I'd surprised him. "But Empath is a villain."

I grinned. "So is Magneto. Who's your favorite character?"

He turned and kept walking. "We better go. We're going to be late."

I hurried to keep up with him, my breaths coming a little easier now. "Have you seen the movies?"

He hugged the comic to his chest. "Of course I have."

"Which one's your favorite?"

"You ask a lot of questions."

"You started it." He didn't respond, so I said, "I like *First Class*."

"The newer movies."

"That movie's hardly new. It's as old as I am!"

"I like the first ones. Before *First Class*."

"Oh...I haven't seen those."

"They're good." He looked at me sideways. "They have Magneto."

"I'll watch them soon. Then maybe we can talk about them? You know, since we apparently live near each other." Adam glanced at me again, and I cringed at how desperate I probably sounded. "Not that, like, I don't have anyone else to talk to." But I'd never had anyone to talk to about Empath or X-Men. I snorted and tried to play it all cool. "I mean, I have *tons* of friends."

Adam gave me another look. "Just not in social studies."

His words surprised me. Even though he'd kept his head down in class, I guess he'd noticed how Bryden and everyone had acted. "No, I guess not there," I said softly.

"They're not very nice, are they?"

Even though I didn't think he'd meant to make me cry, my vision blurred. I stared at the ground while we walked. "No, not really." I squeezed my eyes shut and rubbed them. Cleared my throat. "So do you think you'd want to do that anyway?"

"Do what?"

I tapped the comic book under his arm. "Talk about X-Men."

He looked down, and the corners of his mouth lifted a little. "Sure, okay."

We neared school, and I spotted my two best friends, Dillon and Fernanda (Nan for short).

I waved at them as Adam quickly darted in the opposite direction, his shoulders hunched, head down. "Bye, then!" I called to him.

He glanced back and did a tiny little wave as he moved away from us.

"Hello, marvelous person," Dillon said.

"Hello, marvelous person," I mumbled back absentmindedly, still watching Adam.

The three of us had been greeting one another like that since Dillon became obsessed with this YouTube scientist named Pavel Belsky, who began his videos by saying "Hello, marvelous person" in his thick Russian accent. Dillon's favorite YouTubers were all scientists.

Nan smacked her usual grape gum that constantly got her in trouble at school. "Who was that?"

Adam made his way around a building and disappeared. "His name's Adam. We ran into each other on the way to school. He must live near me." I turned back to my friends. "You know, he just moved here. Maybe we should see if he wants to hang out with us."

Both of their mouths dropped open. It had been only the three of us since kindergarten.

"Why?" Dillon finally asked.

"You know...strength in numbers. And he doesn't know that we're...that we're..."

"Uncool," said Dillon.

"Unpopular," added Nan.

I smiled. "I was thinking more like..." The letters *U, N, C, O, N, V, E, N, T, I, O, N, A, L* illuminated Dillon's and Nan's skin like glowing tattoos. "Unconventional."

Dillon smiled. "Nice. I like it. We're *unconventional.*"

Nan smacked her gum. "Totally."

"He seems weird," said Dillon.

I turned back to where Adam had walked around the building, but of course he wasn't there. "Yeah, he's...different." Different from the Meanie Butt Band. Different in a way I couldn't even understand yet. But I wanted to understand.

Then I looked Dillon up and down, from his Snoopy Vans to his Campbell's tomato soup T-shirt. "And what's wrong with weird, exactly?"

Nan blew a big purple bubble that popped over her pink-glossed lips. "Nothing." She sucked the gum back into her mouth. "Weird is amazing. It's just..." Nan and Dillon glanced at each other, and I could see in the look that they did not like my idea of adding someone to our small group. "We'll think about it." She grabbed Dillon's hand, and they walked off together to their first class.

That annoying rip opened in my chest, letting a tiny bit of my insides out. I wished I could start the day with my friends, but I had to go start it with the Meanie Butt Band. Individual members of the Meanie Butt Band were like a cactus needle in your shoe. Combined, they were like a whole saguaro shoved down your throat.

The Meanie Butt Band consisted of Bryden, Caleb, Valerie, and Emma—the self-appointed most popular kids in school. And I say self-appointed because why else would they ever be popular? No one could've possibly really *liked* them. Dillon, Nan, and I secretly started calling them the Meanie Butt Band last year because it was completely ridiculous and made us giggle whenever we said it. Anytime we could laugh about them seemed to take away a small sliver of their power over us. Just a teeny tiny sliver.

I meandered to my math class, dragging out the time, wishing I could skip it and stay home for first period every day. Bryden and Emma were already sitting in their seats as I shuffled in. "Wheezer's here," Bryden announced.

Mr. Sheffield looked up from his desk. "Bryden," he said in a scolding tone, but then went back to whatever he was grading.

Doing my best to ignore Bryden, I tried to stay calm while I made my way to my seat. *Don't show any emotion. Don't let them know they're getting to you.*

Sesquipedalian. S-E-S-Q-U-I-P-E-D-A-L-I-A-N. Sesquipedalian.

Spelling words helped. Spelling was something I could control.

There was a screeching sound, and then Dr. Delgado, our new principal, began making the morning announcements over the loudspeaker. "Good morning, CCC students!" he said in his overly cheerful voice. I wished I felt as cheerful as he sounded. "Please don't forget about our upcoming dance!"

Emma made wheezing sounds at me as Dr. Delgado continued the announcements, which drowned Emma out to most everyone else.

Obliviscence. O-B-L-I-V-I-S-C-E-N-C-E. Obliviscence.

"Can you even breathe?" whispered Bryden.

Pachydermatous. P-A-C-H-Y-D-E-R-M-A-T-O-U-S. Pachydermatous.

"Maybe she has brain damage from lack of oxygen," whispered Emma.

Stoicism. S-T-O-I-C-I-S-M. Stoicism.

I sank down in my seat, my eyes hot and blurry, but I wouldn't blink. I wouldn't let the tears fall as Dr. Delgado closed the morning announcements in the same way he always did. "And today and every day remember to dream big, listen hard, and be kind to your fellow CCC students!"

Vivisepulture. V-I-V-I-S-E-P-U-L-T-U-R-E. Vivisepulture.

A tear broke free, and I quickly wiped it away
before anyone could see. Spelling helped. But it
wasn't a cure.

chapter 4

Logorrhea.
L-O-G-O-R-R-H-E-A.
Logorrhea.

"Chiaroscurist." Dad shoved a pumpkin ravioli into his mouth.

"Chiaroscurist," I repeated. "C-H-I-A-R-O-S-C-U-R-I-S-T. Chiaroscurist."

Dad smiled. "Excellent."

I popped a ravioli into my mouth and chewed. I wondered what regular ravioli might taste like—made with wheat flour and eggs and cheese and all that. These ones were made with a gluten-free blend and pumpkin filling. They were good, but I bet they paled in comparison to the real thing.

I looked down at my plate and found the letters *C, O, U, N, T, E, R, F, E, I, T* swirling in the sauce.

"What on earth does *chiaroscurist* mean?" Mom asked.

Dad stared at his phone. "A painter who uses light and shade rather than color to create the illusion of volume."

"Wow, that's specific," said Mom.

I already knew the meaning. When Dad said the word, I could see the letters, all blown up with light. I loved words. Loved everything about them. Loved defining them. Loved writing them in a sentence. Loved spelling them. Words had colors, pictures, shapes, and I knew all their letters by heart. For me, words could become their definitions, and objects could become letters, like the sauce on my plate.

Mellifluous flowed on the wind, all floating musical notes and soaring melodies.

Glaucous was pale green. Kind of ugly.

Termagant had long, dark brown hair, beady eyes, and looked down her nose at me. Just like Emma.

Chauvinist had a shaved head and thought he was better than me. Thought he was better than everyone. Just like Bryden.

The school spelling bee was coming up soon, so I was pretty much always practicing. I'd made it to the top two last year, but Daniel Garza had beaten me. I'd lost on *pterodactyl*, spelling it with an *A* instead of an *O* for some stupid reason. I'd had to listen to the Meanie Butts shout pterodactyl sounds at me for the rest of the year (or I guess what they thought were pterodactyl sounds—they sounded more like donkeys) while wildly flapping their arms. Like any of them could ever spell *pterodactyl* in a million years.

I was *not* going to let that happen again this year. This year, I would show *everyone* that I had something they couldn't destroy or take from me. It had been a long time since I misspelled a word, and I would definitely not misspell one while the whole school was watching. After that I would go to the district spelling bee, then county, then regional. And then who knew what might happen—maybe I'd even win the National Spelling Bee because I *never* misspelled. Then I'd be sort of famous, and who had the guts to call a famous person Wheezer? Life would be so much better.

Dad interrupted my little fantasy. "*Logorrhea.*"

I giggled and Mom shook her head. "Did you really just say that at the dinner table?"

"What? It's right here on the spelling list. Not my fault. And I'm sure it doesn't mean what your gross brain is thinking."

"And what am I thinking, exactly?" Mom demanded, biting her lip to keep from smiling.

Dad narrowed his eyes at her. "Oh, you know what it sounds like, or you wouldn't have pretended to be shocked by it."

"So what does it mean, then, smart aleck?" asked Mom.

"Extreme wordiness," Dad read from his phone. "The excessive flow of words."

"Diarrhea of the mouth basically," I said. It didn't make a pretty picture in my head.

Mom slapped the table, but she couldn't keep from laughing. "Stop it, you two! If you say that word again I won't be able to eat anymore."

"Logorrhea. L-O-G-O-R-R-H-E-A. Logorrhea."

"Good," said Dad.

I grinned at Mom. "It's easy because it's spelled like *diarrhea*."

Mom threw her fork down. "I swear if you say that word one more time."

I decided we'd antagonized her enough. "Fine, change of subject. No more diarrhea talk."

Mom shook her head, and Dad snickered.

"So some kid named Adam just moved into the neighborhood," I said. It was a small town, and new people moving in was usually big news. "Do you know anything about his family?"

Mom and Dad looked at each other, then back at me. "Haven't heard anything about a new family moving in," said Mom. "Is he nice?"

"Yeah, he seems pretty nice. He's quiet. He's..." What? Possibly super lonely? Possibly different. Different...like me? Mom and Dad stared at me, waiting for me to complete my sentence, but I took a bite of ravioli instead. "Not that I blame him for being quiet. Must be hard starting at a new school in the middle of the year, and our school probably has the meanest kids in the world."

"That's not true," Mom said. "You have the sweetest two best friends anyone could have."

"They're the *only* nice kids at school."

"There are others," added Dad. "What about He-Whose-Name-We-Do-Not-Speak?"

Dad was talking about Daniel Garza. Despite having beaten me at the spelling bee last year, Daniel was really nice. And unfortunately also as bullied as the rest of us.

"Maybe this Adam's a nice kid, too," said Mom. "And he lives nearby. Maybe you two can become friends."

Sometimes it felt like the three of us shared the same brain, but they didn't need to know that. Instead I told them, "You guys are such optimists."

Dad raised a finger excitedly. "Sanguine. Spell it."

And I did. Because now I could spell everything.

chapter 5

Coterie.
C-O-T-E-R-I-E.
Coterie.

Dillon, Nan, and I hid out in the media center, eating our lunches together. Normally we liked to eat outside, but that haze was back in the air, and it seemed to be getting worse.

Nan kicked me lightly under the table. "There he is, Avalyn."

I turned my head to see Adam skulking into the graphic novel section. Skulking was really the only way to describe his movements, whether he was walking or standing or sitting or browsing books—it was all very skulky.

"You should give him style tips, Dillon," said Nan. "Maybe they'd leave him alone if he wore a different shirt for once."

Every day, the Meanie Butt Band was amping up its attacks on Adam. It had started with calling him Dirt Head. Now they'd begun holding their noses and pretending to sneeze and cough when he was nearby.

I frowned at her. "Are you saying it's his fault?"

"Of course not," she said. "I just feel bad for the guy."

I tugged on Dillon's *Brady Bunch* T-shirt. "I don't know if you should be giving anyone style tips anyway."

Dillon smacked my hand away. "This is what those of us with style call retro, Avalyn."

I snorted. "Which is another word for old."

Adam stood in front of a shelf of books, grabbing one at a time until his arms were full. He glanced at us, and we all quickly looked away. I moved my gaze to the large wall of windows and the haze outside, where kids roamed around with their lunches in hand.

Nan pulled out her phone and held it up. "Oh,

speaking of style, check out my room remodel." Dillon and I oohed and aahed over her new purple walls. "You want to come over after school to see it?"

No matter how many times this happened, I always felt a little sting. It wasn't Nan's fault, but I knew she was only talking to Dillon. She didn't bother asking me anymore because Things I Can't Do: go inside Nan's house because she has two dogs that cover everything in fur; go inside Dillon's house because he has several guinea pigs; play sports (except maybe cornhole or miniature golf, but no thanks); go to the zoo (because animals, hay, dirt, plants); and about a million other things.

"Sure," Dillon said, and tiny drops of my insides drained out.

Nan handed Dillon a cookie. Even though it made me feel bad, it wasn't her fault she didn't hand one to me because Foods I Can't Eat: cow milk (goat milk was allowed, but yuck), wheat, and eggs—which rules out just about everything in the world.

I changed the subject to something that could include me. "Hey, maybe we can get one of our parents to drive us into the city this weekend. I want to go to the bookstore."

Nan took a bite of cookie. "Oh yeah. I want to get a tapestry for my new room." Crumbs flew out of her mouth while she talked.

Dillon gave her a disgusted look and wiped the crumbs from his shirt. "Say it, don't spray it, Nan."

I stared at her. "A tapestry? Isn't that something that's, like, in old castles and stuff?"

Nan took another bite of cookie. "They're back in style."

"You mean they're retro," I said.

Dillon sighed. "That's not retro. That's just super old. Some queen in one of your books must've had a tapestry on her castle wall."

I snorted as Nan grabbed a book out of her backpack. "There are no queens in here," she declared, holding up her copy of *Alcatraz vs. the Evil Librarians*. "Only super tough knights."

"And apparently evil librarians," I added, and we all glanced over at Ms. Lund. She smiled at us, and we burst out laughing. Ms. Lund was the opposite of evil.

"Yeah, let's go shopping," said Dillon. "I need a new pair of shoes."

Nan smacked her lips and licked the crumbs

from around her mouth. "What? A thousand pairs aren't enough?"

Dillon gave us a sheepish grin, his eyes darting from Nan to me. "I need *dancing* shoes."

"No," Nan and I said in unison, then we giggled.

"I want to go that dance, you guys," Dillon whined. "We've never gone to one."

"And we never will." I looked back at Adam, who was now sitting, mostly hidden behind his large stack of books. Seemed deliberate. "I feel bad for him," I said softly.

"Who?" Nan asked, crumbs once again flying and landing on Dillon. His eyes bulged, but she just covered her mouth and laughed. "Sorry."

Dillon shook out his T-shirt. "I don't know how he can even stand to come to school at all."

"Who?" Nan asked again.

I leaned in and whispered to Nan so he wouldn't hear me say his name. "Adam."

"Oh," Nan said. "I feel bad for him too, but I can't help but feel a little relieved that it's taken the focus off us." The focus on us had started as the focus on Dillon. They hated him, and I guess us mostly by association. Mostly.

Then I turned to glance at Adam and saw his eyes peeking over his stack, watching us. I waved at him, and he quickly moved back behind his books.

"What do you think is his deal?" Nan whispered. "Like, why did he even move here?"

"Why would anyone move here?" said Dillon. "As soon as I graduate, I'm gone. Put me on a plane the moment I step off the stage."

Nan rolled her eyes. "We know. You'll leave nothing but a trail of dust all the way to the other side of the country."

Dillon grabbed her hand. "It's going to happen, Nan. Don't you dare make fun of it. Repeat after me." He put his other hand in mine like we were having a séance or something, and I could feel how serious he was. Literally. "Dillon will get a full scholarship to NYU and become a world-changing environmentalist."

Nan and I repeated his words, but I also added, "And you'll figure out how to cure allergies." If Nan was all about fantasy worlds, Dillon was all about the real scientific world. I think I was somewhere in the middle.

"That too." Dillon dropped our hands. "For my bestie." We made silly faces at each other.

I looked back at Adam. "Should we see if he wants to sit with us?" Dillon's and Nan's mouths dropped open as they had when I suggested he join our group before. "Come on, you guys. He has no one." I remembered the feelings I'd gotten from him when he bumped me in class. And when we were out on the street.

Dillon subtly pointed in Adam's direction. "Go right ahead, Avalyn."

"Yeah, have fun," Nan added.

I pushed away from the table and made my way over to Adam. He was hunched down behind his stack, but he glanced up as I neared him. I hadn't seen him walking to or from school again, and I'd wondered if he was avoiding me. Of course, Mom had driven me a couple of times because of the haze, so I really hadn't had too many chances to run into him.

"Did you watch the old movies yet?"

I shifted from foot to foot. I hadn't expected him to speak first, and I'd already worked out what I would say to him on my way over here: *Do you like it here? Is it hotter than where you came from?* Now that was all out the window. "Not yet, but I'm planning to soon."

41

His face fell, and he turned back to his comic book, muttering "Oh" as if he was disappointed.

I quickly sat down next to him and pointed at the comic book on top of his stack. It was all black with two eyes peeking out. "Who's that?"

Adam grabbed the book and set it down between us. "Sooraya Qadir."

"What's her X-Men name?"

Adam didn't answer. Instead, his eyes moved from the book to Nan and Dillon's table, where they were whispering to each other. "Do your friends like X-Men, too?"

They looked at me and Adam and started giggling.

"No, not really." Then I leaned in and said in a low voice, "Sometimes if feels like we don't have a lot in common." I sat back, wondering why I'd even told him that. It was sort of true, but it hurt to say it out loud.

"Then why do you hang out with them?"

Dillon and Nan now had their hands held in small circles in front of their eyes, watching us with pretend binoculars, and I remembered why it didn't matter that we didn't have all the same interests. "I guess...we do have one really important thing in common."

"What?"

I turned back to Adam. "We just really like each other."

Even so, it sometimes hurt that Dillon and Nan seemed to have more things in common with each other than they did with me. Like the X-Men thing. They were totally uninterested, but here was Adam, and he *was* interested. He didn't have to join our small group. Maybe we could have our own separate thing together. I imagined us sharing X-Men comics and watching X-Men movies together, and I saw a sign made of letters over our heads, like a secret club sign: *C, O, T, E, R, I, E.*

He stared at me awhile, like he was deciding what to say next. Finally he spoke. "Her name is Dust."

"What?"

He tapped the comic book with the black cover. "You asked me what Sooraya Qadir's X-Men name is. It's Dust."

"Oh, that's cool. What are her powers?"

"She can turn herself into dust, and she uses that to attack her enemies."

43

"Do you like her?"

"She's okay," Adam said. "I actually like Wind Dancer better."

"Why?"

"Wind Dancer can control dust too, but she doesn't have to turn into anything to do it. She stays herself."

"I think that's better. I wouldn't want to turn into dust. I would make myself cough all the time."

Adam smiled a little. "I guess it's probably easier to stay yourself when you have power."

"Yeah, if anyone doesn't like you the way you are, you can freeze them. Or electrocute them. Or laser beam them!" I brought my hands up to my eyes and pointed my fingers outward like laser beams.

Adam's smile grew. "Right. Like Cyclops."

I dropped my hands and glanced out the window, happy to see the air clearing up. That would make the rest of the day easier. I turned back to Adam, my face serious now. "Or maybe it's harder to totally be yourself when you have power."

He shifted in his seat. "Why?"

"Maybe...maybe you'd need to hide it from people."

44

Adam's smile disappeared. He moved the comic book with Dust on the cover away from me. He opened it slowly and stared down at the pages, at a picture of Sooraya Qadir standing with arms outstretched, the lower half of her body made of swirling dust. "Maybe," he muttered.

The day didn't end up being as clear as I'd hoped.

chapter 6

Turpitude.
T-U-R-P-I-T-U-D-E.
Turpitude.

Language arts was our last class of the day, and it was the best class because it was the only one Nan, Dillon, and I all had together. Unfortunately, the Meanie Butt Band was in there, too.

I sat down at the desk next to Dillon. "Hello, marvelous person."

He looked up. "Hello, marvelous person."

"Hello, marvelous person," Nan mumbled, focused on digging through her backpack. "Aha!" She pulled out a wrinkled paper and worked at peeling off a piece of purple chewed-up gum.

Dillon made a disgusted look. "Is that your personal essay?"

Nan managed to get the gum off and held it on the tip of her thumb in front of her face. "Uh-huh." She popped the gum into her mouth and smacked it loudly.

Dillon and I sort of gag-giggled, and I told her, "You better not let Mr. Griffin see."

Mr. Griffin clapped his hands. He took off his glasses and wiped them on his button-down shirt while he waited for us to calm down. Once the room was silent, he put his glasses back on and announced, "Finishing our personal essays today." He tiredly waved a hand indicating we should get to it.

It was quiet for several minutes, nothing but the sound of scribbling pencils and Mr. Griffin rifling through his desk. He'd been cleaning it out for several days already. Suddenly Bryden called out to him, "Hey, what's another good word for fart?"

Everyone snickered, but Mr. Griffin raised his eyebrows as he moved a stack of papers from his desk to a filing cabinet in the corner. "That's what the thesaurus is for, Bryden. Though I'm not sure why you'd need to include that word for this assignment."

"A loud fart can be life changing," Bryden said, and the class giggled more loudly.

"Flatulate," I said softly.

Flatulate. F-L-A-T-U-L-A-T-E. Flatulate.

Bryden turned to me. "What?"

I set down my pencil. "*Flatulate* is another word for fart."

"Who asked you, Wheezer?" Bryden shot back.

I picked my pencil back up, my cheeks blazing. Why did I speak up in the first place?

"You asked," Dillon said. "She answered. And her name is Avalyn, not Wheezer."

And *this* was why they hated Dillon so much. It had all started in sixth grade when they'd had a group assignment in science and Dillon had been, well, Dillon—a total know-it-all when it came to all things science. He hadn't meant to make them feel like morons. He wasn't a mean person like that. But they would *never* forgive.

Valerie laughed. "Of course someone who probably has a farting problem would know all about farts."

"Everyone farts," said Dillon.

Nan kicked him under the table. "Knock it off," she whispered.

"I don't," said Valerie.

"Yes, you do."

A bunch of people snorted. I looked at Mr. Griffin, but he was opening and shutting the filing cabinet drawers, too distracted to notice the conversation.

Valerie glared at Dillon. "No. I don't."

"Then you have fart breath," said Dillon, and now the whole class was laughing.

"Shut up!" Valerie cried.

"What? If you hold in your farts too long, they get reabsorbed into your body and then come out in your breath. It's science."

Despite how nervous we were about what Dillon was doing, Nan and I couldn't help smiling at each other. Dillon was like an encyclopedia of strange science facts. I wondered if he'd learned this one from Pavel Belsky.

Valerie glared at Dillon, gritting her teeth. "This is why everyone hates you."

I looked up. "Hey."

Valerie shot me such a poisonous look that I moved my eyes back to my desk.

"That's enough fart talk for one day," Mr. Griffin finally said, slipping some papers into a folder and slamming the filing cabinet shut.

Everyone was quiet after that, but Valerie kept glaring over at our table, then whispering to her friends, then they'd all look at us and glare together. My anxiety was sky-high by the time the bell rang.

"Why do you have to be such a know-it-all?" I hissed at Dillon on the way out of class.

"Oh, like it's my fault," he said as we walked down the sidewalk toward the parent pickup line, where I knew Dad would already be waiting for me since it was dusty again today. "I'm so sick of—" Suddenly Dillon tripped forward, his books flying out of his hands and scattering all over the sidewalk. He fell face-first into the pavement.

Nan and I lunged down to grab Dillon, and when I touched him, a sharp pain shot through my face. We lifted him off the ground, and then I saw the blood on his cheek and heard the snickering. I jerked my head toward Valerie and Bryden as they walked past us.

"Whoops," Bryden said snidely. "Sorry."

I watched them walk away, their snickers ringing in my ears. They'd always been jerks, but today was the first time they'd physically hurt Dillon.

Dillon touched his bloody cheek. "He pushed me."

Nan wrapped her arms tightly around him. "We know."

I held on to Dillon, feeling as though my own cheek had been bashed and bloodied, my body flooding with Dillon's embarrassment and anger on top of my own. My eyes moved down to the blood smeared on the pavement. In my mind, it shifted into letters: *T, U, R, P, I, T, U, D, E.*

chapter 7

Implacable.
I-M-P-L-A-C-A-B-L-E.
Implacable.

The dust woke me. I sat up in bed and listened to it crackling against my bedroom window, spackling the whole side of the house. Here's the thing about dust—no matter how much you seal and fill every little nook and cranny and crack, it still gets in.

Pushing myself out of bed, I bent forward and coughed, my lungs constricting. The dust sparkled around my night-light, and I unplugged it so I could try to see better through the window. But it was black as ink, both in my room and outside, the dust having blocked out the moon and stars.

I pressed a hand against my window in the darkness and felt the light vibrations of granules against glass. Such tiny little specks, but I couldn't get away from them. Couldn't stop them. Couldn't keep them out. The grains turned into the letters *I*, *M*, *P*, *L*, *A*, *C*, *A*, *B*, *L*, *E*, battering my window.

"What is happening?" I whispered, then coughed again.

My bedroom light flipped on. I squinted in the sudden brightness at Mom standing in my doorway, all puffy-eyed and groggy, the nebulizer held in one hand, the static electricity in the air causing her sleep-frazzled hair to stick up everywhere. "I heard you."

I nodded and coughed again. "I think we're having another dust storm."

She gazed at the window, which reflected my bedroom like a mirror. "It's so weird. And at night, too."

I got back into bed, and she sat down next to me. She held the mask up, and I put it over my mouth and nose, inhaling slowly and deeply. Mom's head tilted and then fell on top of my pillow as she reached over and turned my lamp off, shocking herself with a loud snapping sound. "Ouch. I wonder if a humidifier would help with this. I'm sick of shocking myself all the time."

"Me too," I said in the dark, my voice muffled under the mask. "You can go back to bed."

She rustled beside me. "That's okay. I'll stay until you're done."

I rolled my eyes, even though I didn't have the benefit of her seeing it. "You really don't have to. I'll be fine. Go to sleep."

"Who needs sleep?" She yawned. "Sleep shmeep. You know, I don't think Dad and I slept well for an entire year after your asthma attack in Oklahoma. I can make it a few minutes." She still acted as though she might get out of the shower one day again and find me all blue and unbreathing.

"That's never going to happen again," I assured her.

"I just wish I knew what was causing this."

I turned and stared at my dark bedroom window, the dust growing louder all the time. "I'm sure it will stop soon."

"It better. Do you think it's climate change?"

"No. It's only a couple of dust storms."

"Could still be climate change. Can't be a coincidence."

"That's a synchronicity. S-Y-N-C-H-R-O-N-I-C-I-T-Y. Synchronicity."

Mom snorted. "You even spell in your sleep."

I smiled in the dark. "I'm not asleep."

Mom's voice was hoarse and slow as she mumbled, "Maybe you're not, but I am."

The continued sounds of the beating dust made me think of Adam. He was still keeping his head down in social studies, and the Meanie Butts had started playing a contest—a contest to see who could get him to raise his head by throwing things at him whenever Mr. Cumberland wasn't looking. They'd thrown paper wads, erasers, and sticks of gum. But still, he hadn't raised his head.

Maybe that was why I'd thought of him. They'd been as implacable with their attacks on him as the dust was being against my window right now. And as class went on, I'd noticed the air outside growing hazier and hazier.

I finished all the medication in my nebulizer and turned it off. Mom was already snoring beside me, so I did my best to curl up next to her and go to sleep while the dust continued battering the house like an intruder desperately trying to break in.

chapter 8

Chutzpah.
C-H-U-T-Z-P-A-H.
Chutzpah.

I had to go to the media center after school the next day to catch up on some work. I was the editor for the yearbook, but it was becoming more and more difficult to get anyone else to do much, so a lot of the work had fallen on me.

Ms. Lund, who was the supervisor for the yearbook committee, waved at me as I pushed through the door. "Hey, Avalyn."

I waved back as I threw my backpack on a table. And then I spotted Adam. He was bent over something, his back to me. I walked to the table and stood over him. "What are you doing?"

He looked up and jumped a little in his seat, quickly covering a scattering of pictures with his arm. "Are you spying on me?"

I took a step back at the accusation. He seemed different, as though something had changed in him. His eyes were full of anger, and I wondered whether the Meanie Butts had finally done something really bad to him, as they'd done to Dillon yesterday.

"Are you okay?" I asked softly.

He stared at me, so much hurt in his eyes. And also surprise. Was he surprised at my concern? Finally, he turned away, mumbling, "I'm fine."

"What are you working on?"

He hunched more over the pictures, shielding them from view while glaring back at me. "Mind your own business."

I didn't have to put up with this, no matter how he was feeling. "Never mind, then." I humphed and flopped down at a nearby table. This stunk. I'd thought maybe I'd finally met someone I could open up to a little, someone who might understand if I told him the thing about myself that I'd never told anyone else. But I guess I was wrong. I let out a loud breath, motorboating my lips. "Geez," I said loudly enough for him to hear.

Adam didn't react, but Ms. Lund jumped in. "Adam's taking pictures for the newspaper and maybe the yearbook," she explained. "I think he'd make a nice addition to the yearbook committee, especially since we're low on candid photographs." Then she walked over to him, and he sat there as Ms. Lund complimented his work and gave him some tips about lighting. I watched out of the corner of my eye as he nodded and listened intently. It irked me that he'd treated me so badly when I'd only tried to be nice to him. He clearly wasn't interested in making friends after all.

"I'm going to go grab a soda," Ms. Lund said. "Okay to leave you two alone for a couple of minutes?"

Adam didn't respond, so I nodded. "Sure." I squinted at him. "Unless he's worried I'll spy on him." But he ignored me, even after Ms. Lund left.

I moved to a computer and started it up. "What's your problem anyway?" I mumbled.

Adam looked up. "Are you talking to me?"

"No, I'm talking to Ms. Lund. She has super hearing. She can hear me from anywhere in the whole school."

Adam scowled. "What are you doing here?" he muttered.

"I'm catching up on yearbook stuff, and I have to wait for my dad to pick me up." I glanced at the big windows. The air looked like you could swim in it. I turned back to Adam. "So why are you really in here? You don't seem like you would ever want to be a part of any committee."

"Why do you say that?"

I snorted. "You don't seem like the committee type."

Adam stared at me with those strangely pale eyes. "You don't know me."

"I know you like X-Men."

His face softened, but he didn't say anything. He turned away from me to sort through his pictures.

My curiosity got the better of me, so I quietly left the computer and crept up behind him, peeking over his shoulder. Most of the pictures were shots of the desert—landscapes and cactuses. I saw he'd taken a picture of the new hedgehog blooms like I had. "Wow, those are good."

He jumped. "I told you to stop spying on me!"

"No, you didn't. You *asked* if I was spying on you. I wasn't before, but this time I was. Your pictures are good. What kind of camera do you use?"

"It's a Canon. No big deal."

"That's a nice picture of Ms. Lund. Do you have a crush on her?"

That got a good reaction out of him. "What? Are you gross?"

"I guess I can be sometimes. One time I had tomato sauce on my shirt all day and didn't even know it, so yeah."

He narrowed his eyes at me. "What's wrong with you?"

"What's wrong with *you*?" I countered. "Why are you being so mean?"

"Why do you keep talking to me?"

"Why are you so suspicious? And why do you ask so many questions?"

"Why—" he started, then stopped himself. "You're weird."

"You're weirder."

We had a bit of a stare down before he finally turned back to his pictures. "You talk too much," he mumbled.

"And you talk too little."

He slapped his hand down and turned back to me. "Why do you have an answer for everything?"

"Ah!" I pointed at him and giggled. "Another question."

I could tell he was trying not to smile, even though he turned away so I couldn't see it. "Knock it off," he said, but his tone had softened.

I went back to the computer just as the door opened. I looked up, expecting to see Ms. Lund, but it was Bryden. And Caleb was with him.

Adam quickly started gathering his photographs into a pile.

Bryden looked from one of us to the other. "Where's Ms. Lund?"

"She just went to get a soda," I said. "She's coming right back."

Bryden smirked and started moving toward Adam. "What are you doing, Dirt Head?"

I could see Adam's hands shaking from all the way across the media center as he attempted to collect his pictures.

"Ms. Lund will be back any second," I repeated, trying to keep my voice calm.

61

Bryden stood over Adam now, staring down, but Adam refused to look up at him. Bryden reached out a hand like he was going to grab Adam's pictures, just as Ms. Lund walked in. "What's up, boys?" she said, and my whole body went limp with relief. "Don't you have baseball practice?"

Bryden finally moved away from Adam and handed Ms. Lund a slip of paper. "Coach wants us to get these baseball books for him."

Ms. Lund looked over the list, then handed it back. "You should know how to find them yourselves."

Bryden groaned. "We don't have much time. We need to get back to practice."

"Finding books in the media center is good practice, too," said Ms. Lund. "Good life skills."

Bryden glared at her, and I couldn't believe how bold he was. I couldn't believe his chutzpah. C-H-U-T-Z-P-A-H. Chutzpah.

But Ms. Lund stared right back, waiting for him to go find his books. I wished I could stand up to him like that, but it was probably a lot easier for an adult. It's not like Bryden would push a teacher. And I couldn't slap Bryden with detention if he didn't back off.

Bryden and Caleb found the books as Adam

slipped his photos into an envelope, which he stuffed into his black backpack. Then he swung the bag over his shoulder and hurried toward the doors.

"Oh, are you leaving already, Adam?" Ms. Lund asked, sitting down at her desk and scanning the first book Caleb had found.

Adam turned, his body pressed against the door, which was just slightly open. "I have to get home."

She pushed the books to Caleb, but her eyes were on Adam. "Is someone picking you up?"

"No...I, um, I..." His eyes darted from Caleb to Bryden to Ms. Lund. "I walk."

Ms. Lund stood and put her hands on her hips. "Okay, well, do you think you can have those photos for me by the end of the week?"

Adam nodded and pushed through the doors, disappearing into the haze.

Caleb stuffed the books into his backpack as Bryden did a little wave at Ms. Lund. Up until now, I hadn't realized waving could be so sarcastic. "See ya," he said, like Ms. Lund was another student and not the librarian. She frowned back at him. Then he and Caleb made their way outside. Where Adam was.

No, not good. Not good at all.

They'd been bullying Adam more every day. I wasn't sure if something they'd done had made Adam act like he was acting today, but I was sure it must've been them. And with the amount of chutzpah Bryden had just shown with Ms. Lund, what might they go out and do to Adam right now?

My heart raced as I grabbed my backpack. "I gotta go, too."

Ms. Lund still had her hands on her hips. "But you haven't even gotten any work done."

I rushed toward the doors, feeling the inhaler in my pocket. "I'll be back tomorrow. Promise." Then I pushed my way out into the growing haze after them.

chapter 9

Phenomenon.
P-H-E-N-O-M-E-N-O-N.
Phenomenon.

It was as I feared. Adam was hurrying, but trying not to look like he was hurrying. Trying not to look afraid, though I could tell he was. I could almost feel his fear all the way across the not-so-empty air that seemed to be getting less empty by the second. Or maybe it was my own fear making my limbs tremble.

Caleb and Bryden were not heading toward the baseball field. They were following Adam.

I ran. "Ms. Lund needs you!" My voice was hoarse. Gasping. My stomach sick. My lungs tight and burning. That rip in my chest began to tear open, but instead of all my insides pouring out, the thick haze was pouring *in*.

Caleb and Bryden stopped and turned, Bryden's narrowed eyes full of suspicion. "Why?"

Adam had heard me too, because he stopped to watch us. I was glad *someone* was watching, even if he was as scared as I was.

"You...forgot a book." I stumbled over my words, making the lie as obvious as my fear.

Caleb crossed his arms. "No, we didn't."

"One...didn't...check out right." More fumbling and stumbling and bumbling.

Bryden grinned, and it was horrible. "Why are you lying, Wheezer?"

I needed a puff of my inhaler, but I didn't want them to know it. "I thought...I thought you had to get back to practice."

Bryden tilted his head, his grin growing into an awful smirk. "I guess we're better liars than you are."

Then they just stood there as I struggled for air. They seemed to have temporarily forgotten about Adam. I guess watching me suffer was more interesting.

Suddenly, Adam was beside me, grabbing my hand. "Let's go."

A shock of electricity exploded when our hands touched, and the surge of feelings that flooded through my body froze me in place.

Air filled me to bursting, tearing my chest wide open and draining all good things out. The only feelings left were fear and anger and loneliness and... something else. Something I hadn't felt from him before. Something that made me feel worse than I'd ever felt in my life. It was a muddy, swampy, dark, stinking feeling—like a flooded hundred-year-old basement. Or a dungeon. It made me want to run home as fast as possible and jump in a scorching-hot shower, hot enough to sting and turn my pale skin bright pink. All these terrible feelings piled on top of my own fear, weighing me down, gluing me to the dirt ground.

"Aw!" Bryden said. "Holding hands. That's so sweet. Wheezer and Dirt Head like each other."

Adam dropped my hand, and the weight of the emotions began lifting. It felt like tearing out a loose tooth—a painful relief that leaves behind a brand-new emptiness that bleeds.

"Let's go now," Adam said.

We turned and walked toward home together

as confidently and casually as possible. I quickly pulled out my inhaler and took a secret puff, but I was too breathless to hold it in for long. The sounds of Bryden's and Caleb's stomping footsteps behind us made my heart race. "Are you two girlfriend and girlfriend?" Bryden shouted.

Why did they always do that? Call boys girls like it was the worst insult in the world. I'd heard them call Dillon a girl a hundred times, just because he wore pink Vans and had lots of colorful buttons all over his backpack.

"Go away!" I called back, nearly running now to keep up with Adam. The air was rapidly growing hazier as the dust picked up around us. It swirled and almost seemed to levitate off the ground. I could feel the electricity building in the air, my hair rising off my head like the dust rising off the ground, as though a magnet were pulling everything upward.

"I'm sorry." I gasped the words out, stopping in place. I took another puff of my inhaler.

Then Bryden was right there, stealing my inhaler out of my hand. Panic exploded inside me. "Please, no." I reached for it. "I need it."

Bryden tossed my inhaler to Caleb. Caleb held

it in front of his body, hesitated, and looked at me. Then to Bryden, and back to me.

"Please," I begged Caleb through my wheezing. I'd often gotten the feeling from Caleb that he was just going along with the others. That his heart wasn't totally in it—the bullying. I hoped it was true right now. "Please."

"Give it back," Adam ordered.

Bryden smirked with satisfaction. "Make him."

Adam leaped for the inhaler, but Caleb moved it out of his reach, holding it high in the thickening air. Suddenly, Bryden seized Adam in a headlock. The air grew even heavier around us, churning and stirring into a vortex. It lifted and spun my hair. My face stung. My eyes watered—from the dust, from fear, from panic.

"Please stop," I croaked though the chaos.

Adam's hands flailed aimlessly around his head, high in the swirling sky, his open-handed slaps weakly landing on Bryden's head, his shoulder, his arm. But Bryden didn't loosen his grip around his neck.

Caleb's head swiveled from Bryden to me and back, his face filled with indecision. I wheezed, my

69

lungs continuing to tighten despite the two puffs I'd had, but I was probably the only one who could hear my whistling breaths over the whirling dust.

Suddenly Adam flung a handful of dirt over his head into Bryden's face. Bryden cried out and let go, wiping his eyes. Caleb got an eyeful of dust next. He dropped the inhaler, and Adam snatched it off the ground. Then Adam gave it to me, his fingers brushing mine. Again, that awful feeling shot through me. I tore my hand away as though I'd touched a hot stove. "Don't touch me!" I shrieked, my eyes irritated and full of tears, my lungs aching for clear air.

He stared at me a moment, his face filled with surprise and confusion. He jerked my backpack. "Come on!" he ordered, moving in the direction of home, but home was still too far away.

Caleb and Bryden were already recovering from the dust, and so I found the last bit of strength I could to run in the direction of the Clear Creek Café.

"Where are you going?" Adam screamed at me. I turned and saw that he was running too, and Caleb and Bryden were right behind him. I didn't have the energy to shout and run at the same time, so I focused on the Clear Creek Café in the distance. People would be there. It would be safe.

I burst inside, and Adam made his way through the door behind me before it had time to close. Then we crouched low, our heads peeking over a window-sill next to the door. Bryden and Caleb stood outside, still rubbing their eyes, their chests heaving. Bryden made his way to the window and peeked inside, and we both dropped to the floor, our backs against the wall. I took a deep puff of my inhaler and held it in as long as possible.

After a minute, we carefully peeked out the window again, but Bryden and Caleb were gone. All that remained were clouds of dust.

"What in the world is going on here?" a woman's voice demanded. We jumped up and spun around. Margie stood behind us, her hands on her wide hips.

"I'm having an asthma attack."

She squinted out the window though her thick-rimmed glasses, tugged on her white apron with the Clear Creek Café logo on the front—two canyon walls with a river running between them. "This darn dust." She shook her head. "Must be that climate change, I suppose." She sounded like Mom. "Should I call someone?"

"No," I said. "I just need a minute." Adam and I sat at the empty breakfast counter. The café was always quiet this time of day between lunch and dinner, but it really wasn't all that busy even during mealtimes. Clear Canyon City didn't have enough people to keep the place filled.

Margie set some ice water on the counter in front of us. "May I actually have a coffee, please?" I asked through wheezing breaths.

Her eyes widened. "Coffee?"

"It helps."

I focused on slowing my breaths.

Slow and deep. Slow and deep.

Adam watched me, his face full of worry, as Margie set a plain white mug on the counter. She filled it with what was probably leftover coffee from this morning's breakfast, and I took small sips. It burned my tongue and tasted bitter and gross.

We sat quietly while Margie tended to the only other customer in the café. She kept glancing at me like she feared I might flop over dead on the counter. I tried to remember how many puffs I'd already taken: at least two outside and one under the window. A fourth puff would be a lot, so I continued focusing on slowing my breaths until they started coming easier.

"That was scary," I finally said. What if I hadn't gotten my inhaler back? What if it hadn't been enough? What if they'd caught us again?

"Yeah," Adam said softly.

I took another small sip of the coffee and swallowed. "Thank you."

Adam tilted his head a little, a questioning look on his face.

"For getting my inhaler back for me."

Adam focused on the glass of ice water in front of him, rubbing a finger over the condensation. "Oh.... What would happen if you didn't have it?"

I took another deep breath, feeling the air fill my lungs. "I could end up in the hospital. I could even die. I almost died once when I was little."

"From your asthma?"

"Yeah. So..." I took another sip of coffee. "Just thank you." I smiled at him. "I guess you kind of saved my life."

Adam's flushed cheeks seemed to turn even pinker. He looked away from me and took a sip of his water. "Thank you, too."

"For what?"

"You wouldn't have been out there in the first place if it weren't for me." He set his glass down, still not looking at me. "Sorry I was rude to you earlier. I had a bad day."

If he'd really been feeling those dark dungeon feelings I'd gotten from him, and I hadn't imagined it, then I definitely believed that he had a bad day. "That's okay. It's been a pretty bad day."

His eyes quickly moved to me and then back to his glass, and he smiled. "It's a little better now."

While we sat there quietly, I replayed the events in my mind—from Bryden stealing my inhaler to Bryden holding Adam in a headlock. Something about it didn't make sense.

"How did you do that?" I finally asked.

"What?"

"How did you get that dirt to throw in their faces?"

He hesitated for a second before answering. "I

just reached down and grabbed it. It's not like there's a shortage around here."

"No. You didn't. You couldn't. He had you in a headlock."

"I grabbed it earlier," he said. "I already had it in my hand."

We stared at each other a second before he looked away. I wanted to keep pressing him, but I didn't. Because I knew he hadn't had the dirt in his hand. The same hand that had thrown the dirt had been in my hand seconds before. His hand had been in mine, and neither hand touched the ground after that. They'd flailed in the thick air. They'd slapped at Bryden. Open-handed slaps. Not closed-fist punches.

It was like the recent dust storms. Like me. Another anomaly.

I put my coffee down and opened my hand, running a finger over my palm, which was smeared with dirt from the second time Adam had grabbed it. When I'd ripped away from him as though he were a wasp stinging me.

He'd had two handfuls of dirt when he needed it,

and my mind found the letters across my skin: *P, H, E, N, O, M, E, N, O, N.*

It was as though Adam had pulled dust out of the air, siphoned it right out of the dust devil swirling around us. Just like Wind Dancer.

Because I knew his hands never touched the ground.

chapter 10

Camaraderie.
C-A-M-A-R-A-D-E-R-I-E.
Camaraderie.

Weekends were the best. Weekends meant no school and no Bryden or Valerie or Emma or Caleb calling me Wheezer or pushing Dillon down or saying mean Spanish words in terrible accents to Nan. Lately it also meant escaping the dust because Clear Canyon City had been a lot dustier than all the areas surrounding it, which made absolutely no sense at all. Because geography.

Dad took Nan, Dillon, and me shopping in Phoenix. We stopped at the bookstore for me, the home store for Nan's tapestry, and the shoe store for Dillon.

Despite having *city* in its name, Clear Canyon City had almost nothing—just the café and a bar and a tiny little grocery store that carried mostly canned and boxed food, much of which was usually expired.

After we finished our shopping, we went to a movie, where I could actually share candy with my friends, as long as they bought the right ones, which they always did. You'd think I could have candy like Red Vines and Twizzlers, but nope. Even those had wheat in them. And of course all chocolate bars were a total no go. But I could have Skittles, Starburst, and Nerds, though we wouldn't be caught dead eating Nerds at school after the day someone shouted at us, "Look! Nerds eating Nerds!"

Then Dillon and Nan came home with me for a sleepover. Some people may have found it odd that our parents let Dillon sleep over, but the three of us had been best friends since kindergarten. Dillon could've been our brother.

After we got home, Dillon put on his new shoes and stood in front of my closet mirror. "I'm thinking…" He scratched his head. "I'm thinking the pineapple shirt with these."

Nan looked up at him from the floor, where she

was painting her toenails purple. "For what?" She blew on her foot.

Dillon whirled and began swinging his arms wildly.

I was wiping down my windowsill and furniture with a damp paper towel; I couldn't let the dust build or I'd be up all night coughing, which would keep Dillon and Nan awake. I threw the paper towel in the garbage can. "Why are you flossing?"

Nan stopped blowing on her nails, her mouth frozen in a pucker. She started slowly shaking her head. "We already told you we're not going to that dance."

"Oh no," I chimed in. "No way."

Dillon stopped his flossing and sulked over to my freshly wiped dresser, his face all droopy and defeated. He began rummaging through the comic books I'd bought on our shopping trip. "*Still* into X-Men. Huh, Avalyn?"

I had to admit, the way he said that *still* stung, but I acted casual. "I guess."

Nan jumped up and snatched a comic book from the stack on my dresser. "I don't get it." She lay back on my bed, her arms fully extended toward the ceiling, the book open in her hands. Compared to Nan's new ornate bed (which I'd only seen pictures of), mine was totally boring—plain white sheets, white comforter, white pillows, and a light gray padded headboard. Sometimes I felt sort of drab compared to my two friends. Nan was all purple walls and flowery quilts and colorful tapestries. Dillon was perfectly styled hair and retro T-shirts and a thousand pairs of Vans in every pattern and color imaginable. I didn't know how to be anything but white walls and plain jeans.

"You don't have to get it." I tried not to let the annoyance, the offense, show in my voice. After all, we didn't have to be into all the same things. And Adam got it. Maybe he got it too well.

Nan twisted up her face. "This stuff is weird. This guy is called Goldballs." She snickered. "What are his powers?"

"I don't think I even want to know," said Dillon, but he lay down next to Nan and looked up at the comic book as if he did want to know after all.

"He lays golden eggs," I explained. "But they come out of his chest."

Dillon burst out laughing. "Then why is he called Goldballs?"

Nan side-eyed him, their heads smooshed together under the comic book. "I told you this stuff was weird." She muttered it under her breath like it was a secret between them I wasn't supposed to hear.

My chest suddenly ached with emptiness, but I forced a smile. "I know, right? I think they actually changed his name to Egg in later comics, but Gold-eggs would've been even better. You want to know his real name?" They both looked up at me with wide eyes. "It's Fabio."

They laughed, and I lay down next to them to look at the comic. "Do you think it could be possible, though?" I asked softly.

Dillon flipped the page. "What? That a dude named Fabio could shoot golden eggs out of his chest? Doubtful."

I giggled. "No. You know...to have a mutation that could give you some kind of power?"

"Some people have higher blood oxygen levels." Dillon's eyes scanned the page. "So they can hold their breath longer. And some people have genes that give them stronger muscles."

"I don't know if I'd consider that a power," said Nan.

I pressed him further. "What about something like what Professor X and Jean Grey have? I think it's called telepathy?"

"They read people's minds?" said Dillon.

"Yeah, but they can also move things with their minds."

"Ah." Dillon raised a finger. "You mean telekinesis."

"Yes, telekinesis. Do you think that's possible?"

We all three sat up, and Nan tossed the comic book on the bed. "That stuff is too weird for me." She ran a hand through her long dark hair. "I think I'll stick with Maya." *Maya and the Rising Dark* was Nan's latest fantasy obsession. "Have I told you that you remind me of Frankie?" Her question was aimed at Dillon.

"Yes," we both said.

"Like a hundred times," Dillon added.

Nan flipped her hair back. "Frankie's obsessed with science, too."

"We know," I said. When Nan was into a good fantasy story, she talked about it a lot. "So, *do* you?" I asked Dillon.

"Do I what?"

I turned to him, sitting cross-legged on the bed. "Think telekinesis is possible?"

Dillon seemed to seriously consider the question. "Well, our brain does send electrical signals, so I think telepathy would be more likely than telekinesis. And there *are* people who can access more of their brains than most people, like geniuses and savants and people like that."

"Oh, like me," said Nan.

Dillon looked at her doubtfully. "There's a big difference between being a genius and just being smart."

Nan's face fell and she shot him a dirty look. "I guess that rules you out too, then. Your brain is too small."

"It has nothing to do with brain size. I'm talking about people who can use more of their brain than the rest of us. So maybe there's a part of the brain that could send signals outside the body to another person's brain, but most people can't access it. We do have technology now that can read brain signals and use them to control machines."

I grabbed one of my white pillows and hugged it over my crossed legs. "Like a robot we can control with our minds?"

Dillon moved his arm in a sort of jerking motion. "Yeah, like a robotic arm and stuff like that."

"What about emotions?" I squeezed one corner of my pillow. "Are those made of electricity? And could someone…maybe only receive the signals instead of sending them?"

Nan scrunched up her face. "My mom says all my emotions are made of puberty hormones."

"Hormones are chemicals," said Dillon. "Not electricity. But our emotions *are* tied to our brains, so I suppose it could be possible. I wouldn't rule it out. Electricity needs a conductor, though, so at the very least I'd think you'd need to be touching the person or have something conductive, like water or a piece of metal, connecting you to transmit the signals."

Touching the person.

I threw my pillow down. "Let's try it."

Dillon raised an eyebrow. "You want to try telepathy?"

Nan shook her head and tapped her temple. "You don't want to know what's going on in here."

Dillon placed his hands on either side of her head. "I bet it's scary in there, Nan." He closed his eyes as if he were reading her mind. Then he began making scared noises. "No...no, no, no. Make it stop. It's all purple. And there are faeries. And elves. And...My Little Pony!"

Nan laughed and shoved him away.

Dillon collapsed on the bed, gasping out, "I'm traumatized now."

"Seriously, you guys." I got off the bed. "Let's try it."

They looked at each other. "How are we supposed to try it?" asked Dillon.

"Like you said, we need a conductor. Or to be touching." The three of us got down on the floor in a tight circle and pressed our heads together. I figured the shorter the distance the electrical signals had to travel, the better it would work.

"What now?" asked Nan.

"Think of something," I said. "Something simple."

We all sat quietly for a minute, our heads smooshed together, and the feelings I got from them warmed my chest. That was the thing about friendship—when you knew for a fact someone truly loved you, it was a lot easier to forgive the small things. It was as if I could feel the letters C, A, M, A, R, A, D, E, R, I, E in their touch.

"That's mean, Nan," said Dillon.

"What's mean?" I asked.

"She's thinking this is stupid."

Nan huffed. "I was not. I was thinking I have to pee. You're thinking you really want to get home and play with your circuit board."

"You know I don't play with my circuit board on Saturdays. Saturday is for K'nex only."

Just then we heard my bedroom door open. Dad cleared his throat, but we kept staring down, our heads pressed together, concentrating.

"Do I even want to know what's going on in here?" asked Dad.

"Science experiment," I said.

"What kind of—"

I shushed Dad before he could keep speaking.

"Are you—"

Now all three of us shushed him.

"I'm getting something," Dillon said. "Oh, wait... am I? Yes. I'm definitely getting something. Avalyn is annoyed with her dad for interrupting our science experiment." The three of us giggled, and I heard Dad sigh. "Also, she wants him to bring us the fake Oreos from the kitchen. And the tortilla chips."

"Is this science experiment about reading minds?" asked Dad.

"I'm getting something, too," said Nan. "Avalyn wishes her dad would stop asking questions and hurry. And also bring the Dr Pepper."

We didn't see the look on his face as he left because our heads were still pressed together, the three of us snorting and staring at the carpet. I couldn't hear any thoughts, but my chest was completely full now. No more empty spaces from earlier.

chapter 11

Idiosyncrasy.
I-D-I-O-S-Y-N-C-R-A-S-Y.
Idiosyncrasy.

I lay awake that night, Nan snoring softly beside me. She and Dillon had finally conked out after we all consumed a ridiculous amount of sugar. I'd dozed for a little while, but the dust woke me. It had started as a light sprinkling sound, and at first I'd thought it was raining. That would've been amazing. I was already fantasizing about how the air would smell in the morning. How the rain would clean and clear away the growing haze. The cool crispness of it all.

But the hum outside kept getting louder and louder until it drowned out the white noise of the new air filter Dad had bought me while we were in town. When the dust started pummeling the house like a flock of angry woodpeckers determined to peck through the walls, I knew it wasn't rain.

I pushed myself up in bed, and Nan shifted and groaned beside me. "What are you doing?" she mumbled.

"I can't sleep," I whispered, my lungs tightening. "There's a bad dust storm outside."

Nan pushed herself up next to me, suddenly more alert. "Whoa. It sounds scary."

Dillon shushed us from his sleeping bag. "I'm trying to sleep," he whined.

Nan ignored him. "I've never heard anything like it."

I gazed at her in the dark, my night-light barely illuminating her face, making her brown eyes look like small black caves. "We had one the other night. Didn't you hear it?"

"I guess I slept through it. I might have slept through this one if you hadn't gotten up."

"Maybe it didn't hit your house as hard," I said. Nan's family lived about five miles to the north.

Dillon rolled around dramatically in his sleeping

bag. "*Maybe* you two should shut up and go back to sleep."

Nan flopped back down on the bed. "Okay, Mr. Crabby Pants."

"I don't see why I always have to sleep on the floor anyway," he complained, punching his pillow and making huffing sounds.

"Because you're the smallest and weakest, and we can beat you up," said Nan.

I pushed myself out of bed and walked to the window. "You don't want to sleep next to Nan anyway." I put my hand against the rattling glass, wondering if it was possible for dust to sand a window away. It made me think of sea glass. "She kicks and punches me all night long."

She grunted. "And you snore, Avalyn."

I knew that was true. Sleep was becoming more difficult every night because of how congested I was getting. I'd wake up with my throat raw and sinuses swollen and hurting, my chest full of phlegm.

Dillon stood up and walked to the window. "Well, forget about sleep." His blond hair stuck up every which way. For a second, he looked like he did back in kindergarten. Sometimes I wished the three of us *could* be back in kindergarten, still playing dress-up and hide-and-seek together. The worst bullying back then was someone sticking a tongue out at us or calling us poopy pants.

"Do you think if the dust blew hard enough, it could make a hole in my window?" I asked him.

"That would take a long time."

"How long does it take to make a piece of sea glass?"

"Years. And that sand is rubbing the glass all the time. The dust could never blow here long enough and hard enough to sand through the glass. It will stop soon."

I still had my hand pressed against the window, the vibrations so strong they tickled my fingers. "How do you know it will stop?"

He grabbed his sleep-mussed hair and smoothed it down. "Because it's never done this before and it's not normal. I don't know what's causing it, but it's definitely not normal."

"An idiosyncrasy. I-D-I-O-S-Y-N-C-R-A-S-Y. Idiosyncrasy."

"Exactly. Some sort of weird blip in the weather."

I coughed. "That's good."

Dillon drew his eyebrows together in concern. "It will be okay, Avalyn."

But this was the third dust storm already this year. I didn't think we'd had three bad dust storms in the whole ten years before.

Even after we all went back to bed, and both Nan and Dillon were sleeping soundly again, I couldn't rest. Even after Mom gave me a breathing treatment in the living room. Even after the sun began to rise and the dust faded from the sound of angry woodpeckers back to the sound of light sprinkling rain and, finally, to total silence. Even then, I lay awake staring at my ceiling, the dust sparkling across the room in a beam of morning light.

Nan had said the dust sounded scary. But she had no idea what real fear felt like.

chapter 12

Intransigent.
I-N-T-R-A-N-S-I-G-E-N-T.
Intransigent.

"Oh my gosh, Mom!" I pushed the bandana away. We were sitting in front of school. She'd had to drive me because that haze was back. Again. "There's no way in you-know-where I'm wearing that bandana to school."

"But you love WordGirl."

Yeah, I did. But I didn't need WordGirl, her fist jutting out in front of her like she was flying right out of my mouth, plastered on my face for all to see.

Mom dropped the WordGirl bandana on her lap. "I just thought it would be better than going back to masks." She ran a hand through her hair and sighed. "Everyone's tired of those."

I looked down at the bandana and softened my tone. "It was a nice idea. Just…no one else at school wears a bandana over their mouth."

"This dust isn't letting up. It only seems to be getting worse." Her face brightened. "If you're too embarrassed to wear WordGirl, how about a Dog Man one, then? Or maybe I could order a Baby-Sitters Club bandana? Everybody loves those, right?"

I stared at her. How could she not understand that there was no way I would ever wear any kind of bandana over my face at school like I was going out to rustle cattle or something?

Mom stared right back. "Isn't being able to breathe more important than being cool, Avalyn?"

This wasn't about being cool. This was about doing anything I could to avoid making myself a target. "Mother," I said in my deepest voice.

She drew in a breath and crossed her arms. "Daughter."

"I would rather stay home than wear that bandana to school. I would rather eat a real mud pie than wear that bandana to school. I would rather eat a real *cow* pie."

"Oh really? Would you also rather be dead?"

I snorted and rolled my eyes. "You are so dramatic."

"Am I? Am I really? Why don't we call the Tulsa hospital and ask how dramatic I'm being?"

I didn't think it was possible to roll my eyes any harder, but I somehow managed it. Why did that always have to get brought up? It was ten years ago.

Mom said, "You're being so...What's a good word for what you're being?"

"Intransigent?"

"What does that mean?"

"Stubborn."

"Yes, that's perfect. How do you spell it?"

"Intransigent. I-N-T-R-A-N-S-I-G-E-N-T. Intransigent."

Mom narrowed her eyes at me. "Good. I'll need that word a lot."

I snatched the bandana from her lap. "I'll hold on to it for emergencies."

"I suppose I'll accept that compromise. Keep it safe and clean and within arm's reach."

I stuffed it into my shorts pocket and saluted her. "Yes, ma'am."

Mom reached over and rustled my hair. "Don't you 'yes, ma'am' me."

"Yes, madam."

Mom bit back a smile and shoved my arm playfully. "Get outta here."

I stepped out of the car and slammed the door, then turned around and knocked on the window. Mom rolled it down.

"Yes, gentlewoman."

Mom laughed and waved a hand. "Get lost, lady."

I snickered as I hurried toward class, the bandana safely tucked deep in my pocket where no one could see it. Yeah, it was a little tough to breathe, but I would have to be fully drowning in dust, seconds away from certain death, to put that thing on my face at school.

Later, I tried to catch Adam's attention as he blew past me to his seat in social studies, but he didn't even glance in my direction. As he'd done every day since he got to CCC Middle School, he hurried to his seat and put his head down on folded arms.

I hadn't gotten to talk to him since the day of the dust devil, and I wasn't even sure what I would say when I did get to talk to him. I knew I couldn't outright ask him if he'd had something to do with it. If he was...like me. Different. Could he sense that I was different, too? Is that why he'd looked at me that first day in class? I didn't know why, but I was starting to feel that Adam was the answer to all the questions I'd had about myself and whether I could really do what I always thought I could do. The final confirmation that I wasn't bonkers.

But what if I'd been wrong about what I saw? I'd been so certain at first. Now I was getting all confused. I kept replaying what had happened over and over in my mind. What if he really did have the dirt in his hand from the start? Then we'd both think I was totally bonkers.

I heard snickering and turned to see Bryden scratching his head. Then Emma was scratching her head, too, while glaring at Adam. They began whispering to everyone around them, and I made out a word in all the mutterings: *lice*.

They were telling everyone Adam had lice.

I thought about saying something—telling them

to knock it off. Telling them he didn't have lice. But that would just put the focus back on me, so I kept quiet.

Adam didn't lift his head all through class again, even though the head scratching and whispers continued while we watched a documentary about the art of the Renaissance period. Actually, no one was watching the documentary. The Meanie Butts were too busy tormenting Adam, and I was too busy watching the window—watching the air grow thicker with every whisper. With every head scratch.

By the time social studies ended, and Adam ran outside without saying anything to me, my lungs were feeling the growing dust in the air, so I made my way to the nurse's office. Ms. Imani had all the drawers in her desk open when I walked in. She looked up and smiled. Ms. Imani always wore fun scrubs at school, and today they were bright blue with colorful seahorses all over them.

Ms. Imani had been the nurse since I started middle school, and over the last couple of years, we'd spent a lot of time together. She had backups of all my medications, extra rescue inhalers, and even

EpiPens on hand, although I'd never had to use an EpiPen before. She also had a nebulizer.

"Hey, Avalyn," she said. "Everything okay?"

I wheezed. "Just having a tough time breathing today."

She made an exasperated sound. "This dust, no doubt," she complained. "You want me to call your dad?"

I shook my head. "I was hoping to do a breathing treatment and see if that helps."

"Sure thing." She slammed the drawers shut. "I'll find that super expensive digital thermometer later." She rolled her eyes and tucked a long dark braid behind her ear. "I swear, Avalyn, if my head weren't screwed on today, it would be rolling down the hallway."

I smiled as she went to the closet and grabbed my nebulizer, placing it on the counter next to the sink. I waited on the little bed while she pulled out the small plastic vial of medication, twisted the top off, and squeezed it into the nebulizer cup until the medication was gone, tossing the empty package into a garbage can.

"So how's everything going?" she asked, attaching the T-piece.

I kicked my feet. "Okay, same as always."

She walked back over to the closet and rummaged around. "Now where's the stinking mask?" she huffed.

"It's okay. The mouthpiece is fine if you have it."

"Speaking of masks," she said, still searching, knocking over bottles and shoving towels aside, "you might want to consider having your parents pick you up some, until this dust clears. Some disposable N95s would probably be fine."

I groaned.

"I know, I know. But I think it would really help with your breathing."

I didn't mention the WordGirl bandana in my pocket. I worried Ms. Imani would be like *Why on earth aren't you wearing it?* and then I would somehow have to explain the whole cattle rustling thing.

She sighed. "All right. Add that to the list of things I can't find today." She carried the nebulizer over to the bed, then plugged it into an outlet. "I cannot wait for summer," she muttered. "This year has felt eternal. Do you have any summer plans?"

"Not really." I would be thrilled to get away from school, of course, but the heat was always awful. No matter how long we'd lived here, I could never get used to the summer heat. I wished we had a pool. A *real* pool, not a leaky blow-up play pool. Nan was having a real pool built at her house, and Dillon and I were counting down the days until we could finally use it. "Do you?"

She attached the mouthpiece and reservoir tube to the T-piece. "My boyfriend is taking me to Tahiti."

I smiled, but I was totally weirded out about the fact that Ms. Imani had a boyfriend. Of course I knew teachers had lives outside of school; it was just strange to think about it. "That's cool. I've never even been out of the country." I'd hardly ever been outside of Arizona since we moved here.

"Me neither," she squealed, handing me the mouthpiece, which I slipped into my mouth. She turned the nebulizer on, and steam began pouring out of the reservoir tube. I breathed, taking the medication deep into my tired lungs.

Ms. Imani patted my back. "Good?"

I nodded, not sure if the warmth filling up my chest was from only the medication or also from Ms. Imani. Probably both.

She leaned in and, over the drone of the nebulizer, whispered, "I think he might propose to me," like it was a big secret between us.

I lifted my fingers that weren't holding the mouthpiece and crossed them, and she laughed.

Even though I almost only ever saw Ms. Imani when I was sick, I was always glad to see her.

chapter 13

Anathema.
A-N-A-T-H-E-M-A.
Anathema.

After school, Dad was stuck in a terrible traffic jam from an accident on the freeway, so I went to the media center to wait, but Ms. Lund had already closed up for the day. I definitely didn't want to wait in the office, so I opened our group chat.

> **Avalyn:** Air's not too bad right now. Going to walk home.

> **Dad:** Are you sure? Looks a bit hazy from here.

Avalyn: Feeling good. Had a breathing treatment with Ms. Imani. Plus, I really want to try out my cool new bandana.

Dad: Lol! Right.

Dad: You have your inhaler?

Avalyn: Of course.

Mom: I saw that joke about the bandana.

Avalyn: Who's joking? Love you.

Avalyn: And my bandana.

Mom: 🙄

Dad: Text us when you get home.

I slipped the bandana over my nose and mouth, slung my backpack over my shoulder, and set out toward home. As I walked along the quiet dirt road, I heard an echo of footsteps behind me. I stopped and turned. It was Adam. And then I remembered my face was covered and quickly ripped the bandana off and shoved it into my shorts pocket.

"What was that?" he asked as he neared me. I was surprised he was talking to me after he totally ignored me in social studies. But then again, I could also understand why he didn't want to talk when the Meanie Butts were around.

"Nothing."

"It looked like a bandana."

"Yeah, I guess."

"What was on it?"

I sheepishly took it from my pocket and opened it up so Adam could see the picture of WordGirl.

He studied the bandana. "What's that?"

I sighed. "It's WordGirl."

"She looks like a superhero."

"She is."

"What are her superpowers?"

I stuffed the bandana back in my pocket. "She fights bad guys with her monkey and her..." I kicked my toe into the dirt road. "Amazing vocabulary skills," I mumbled.

Adam grinned. "It looks like she's flying."

"Yeah, she can also fly." I said it like that super-power paled in comparison to her vocabulary skills.

"Do you need to wear it?"

I didn't know how to answer that question. *Should* I wear it? Probably yes. But did I *need* to wear it? Also probably yes. But why wasn't I wearing it? That part was tough to explain. Adam had his camera slung around his neck and a comic gripped under his arm. "Is that your Canon?" I asked.

He lifted it to show me. "Yes."

I held it a moment, the strap still around Adam's neck, turning it over. "Where's the screen?"

"It's not digital," he explained. "It uses real film."

I handed the camera back to him. "Have you been taking pictures for the yearbook?"

He shrugged. "I figure I should have it with me in case I see something."

"Something for the yearbook?"

"No. Just like . . . something I want to remember."

"Like what?" I repeated.

His smile grew. "You really do ask a lot of questions."

"I guess I'm just a curious person. You want to walk together?"

"Sure." He acted all casual. I was dying to know how he really felt about it, but I was too scared to touch him and find out. His mood was so up and down.

We walked quietly along the dirt road together until Adam asked, "So did you watch the old X-Men movies yet?"

"No, I've been really busy."

"Busy with what?"

"The spelling bee? It's coming up."

Adam nodded but didn't ask any more about it. A snake slithered across the road in front of us, and he jumped back.

"It's just a gopher snake. Don't you have gopher snakes where you come from?" I was hoping he'd say something about where he'd come from or why he'd moved here, but he just shook his head. So I asked another question that I hoped would tell me something important about him. "Why do you like X-Men so much?"

"I don't know. Why do you?"

"I guess I like that they have these mutations. But instead of the mutations hurting them, they give them cool powers."

"You mean they're not like your asthma."

I hadn't really been thinking of that. "I guess." I followed him quietly for a while before finally building up the courage to ask, "Do you think you have some kind of mutation?"

Adam stopped and stared at me like I'd just let out a huge fart or something. "Are you serious?"

"Yeah, I mean," I stammered, "I think I have one." I'd never told anyone, not even Mom and Dad, about how I thought I could feel other people's emotions. That I was possibly like Empath. I wasn't sure how people would react. If they'd believe me. And I honestly wasn't 100 percent sure I wasn't simply imagining it all the time. The emotions felt completely real, but could they have been coming from only me?

"Your asthma?"

"No." I made a snap decision not to tell him either. "Spelling."

I was still getting that fart look. "You think spelling is your mutation?" Then his face broke into a smirk. "Oh, like WordGirl."

I felt so stupid. "Yeah, I guess sort of like Word-Girl. But her superpower is vocabulary, and mine is spelling. Though I guess I do also know most of the definitions. It helps sometimes to know what a word means. Where it came from. And sometimes..."

"Sometimes what?"

"Well...I guess I spell so much that I can sometimes see letters in things." I pointed at a puffy cloud in the sky. "Like, that sort of looks like a cow, don't you think?"

Adam glanced upward. "I guess."

"So my brain finds letters instead of shapes. I guess letters are also shapes. I mean, they're not really there or anything. I just think about spelling so much that I can see words in things. I guess that's how it works." I was rambling.

"That's weird."

I grimaced. If he thought that was weird, I definitely didn't want to tell him about the feelings thing.

"I'm not very good at spelling," said Adam. "I always misspell *necessary.*"

"Necessary? That's an easy word."

"I can never remember if it's two *C*s or two *S*s."

"Necessary," I said. "N-E-C-E-S-S-A-R-Y. Necessary."

Adam scrunched his eyebrows, and I worried I'd just been show-offy and made him feel bad.

"Anyway," he said, "spelling isn't a mutation, and it can't be a superpower." He continued walking.

"Why not?" I asked, catching up to him.

"Because superheroes use their superpowers for good. To help people. You said yourself WordGirl uses her vocabulary skills to fight bad guys. I bet you just use spelling to help yourself."

Well, that kind of stung, even if it was true. I wanted to win the spelling bee. For myself. Who else would I want to win it for? "I guess," I muttered. "Then what about villain superpowers?"

"Okay, fine. Superpowers aren't always used for good. If they use them to hurt people, they're villains."

"So don't tell me spelling can't be a superpower." I glared at him. "I could spell something right now that would hurt you big time."

Something sparked in his pale eyes that I hadn't seen before. "Do it, then," he challenged.

Of course my mind went totally blank for way too long. I squinted at him. "You look like a…like an affenpinscher. A-F-F-E-N-P-I-N-S-C-H-E-R. Affenpinscher."

"What's that?"

"A scruffy dog."

He smiled again. "You're right. That did hurt big time. Maybe you *can* be a villain."

That made me wonder if villains ever thought of themselves as villains. Or did they always see themselves as the heroes of the story? "Which X-Man do you think you're the most like?" I asked.

"None of them."

I waited for him to ask me the same question, but of course he didn't. "I sometimes think I'm kind of like Rogue."

He looked at me side-eyed. "I would've thought you'd be most like WordGirl."

And this was why I would never wear that bandana in public again. Maybe I'd get some N95 masks like Ms. Imani suggested. "She's not an X-Man," I said, finding it difficult to hide my annoyance.

"I didn't realize Rogue was a super speller."

"She's not," I said. "At least not that I know of."

"Rogue started as a villain."

"Like me—the spelling villain."

"Rogue's one of the main characters in the first movie, so you should really watch it."

"Hey, maybe we could watch it together. Do you have any pets?"

Adam gave me a confused look. "No, why?"

"That's great! Because I could come to your hou—"

Adam suddenly stopped and whirled to me, his cheeks pink. "No!"

I startled and took a step back at his outburst. "Sorry," I whispered.

Adam seemed to calm a little, and his face softened. "It's not you. It's just that I'm not allowed to have people over."

I tilted my head at him and stepped closer. "Your parents don't let you have friends over?"

He continued walking. "I don't live with my parents."

This news surprised me. "Oh. Who do you—"

But Adam interrupted me before I could finish the question. "Why do you think you're like Rogue? Because you're both villains?" He lifted the corner of his mouth a little.

He hadn't let me finish my question. Did he not want me to know who he lived with? That was weird. And why couldn't he have friends over? His smile seemed as forced as his change of subject, but I decided not to push the issue.

"Rogue can't have human contact," I said. "She hurts people, can even kill them, just by touching them. She must be really lonely." I didn't tell him I mostly felt like her because she could absorb things from people through skin-to-skin contact—their memories, strength, and even personality traits. Sort of like how it felt for me to absorb people's emotions by touching them. But I didn't tell Adam that because he would probably give me the fart look again.

"I guess," he said.

"Sometimes I feel like that," I continued. "Like, I can't go inside my best friends' houses because they have animals and other things that can hurt me." I knew Adam could relate to my feelings of loneliness. I'd never felt such loneliness from another person before, and I wondered if he might open up to me about it.

"Isn't your situation sort of reversed, then?" he asked. "*You're* the one who's hurt by touching things?"

I bit my lip. "I just think we probably have some of the same feelings."

"You'd be pretty cool if you were actually like Rogue. She's one of the most powerful X-Men. Not only can she absorb people's powers, but she absorbs their life force, too, which can kill them. I wish I had her mutation."

"Why?" I smirked. "So you could steal my spelling powers?"

But Adam didn't smile. Whatever small spark I'd seen in him got suddenly snuffed out, and the haze that had been clearing from the air seemed to come back. Even though I was scared of what he was feeling, I desperately wanted to know if there was some connection. That I wasn't imagining things. And so I allowed my arm brush his.

That dark dungeon feeling filled my body, but it wasn't as strong. It was as though Adam had figured out a way to close the door on the dungeon. Lock it. Maybe even move one of those secret bookcase entrances over it so no one could find it. Also, there was another feeling overtaking it.

My chest tore open, letting every bit of warmth and kindness and love pour out in a sad stream that trailed behind me on the dirt as we walked. There was only one word to describe what I was feeling, and the letters were like dull, rusty needles pricking my cold, vacant insides.

A attacked.

N nicked.

A ached.

T tortured.

H hurt.

E exploded.

M maimed.

A annihilated.

Anathema. A-N-A-T-H-E-M-A. Anathema.

"No." Even though Adam's voice was quiet, it shook with intensity. "So some people would die when they touch me."

chapter 14

Putrefaction.
P-U-T-R-E-F-A-C-T-I-O-N.
Putrefaction.

"You better go inside," Adam said.

I nodded as I turned away from him, then shuffled up my front walkway and through the front door, closing it gently behind me. I hadn't uttered another word to him after what he said about Rogue.

I went to the living room window and watched as he walked away, his words still pounding in my head, the pricking of the rusty needles fading. I shivered, even though it was warm both outside and inside the house.

So some people would die when they touch me.

It hit me that I didn't truly know Adam. He knew where I lived and what I liked and who my friends were, but I still didn't really know anything about him except that he liked X-Men and taking pictures. That the first time he bumped me I'd felt something totally different from him than I'd ever felt from another person in my whole life. That he was possibly hiding something terrible down in that dungeon inside of him.

And that he apparently wanted someone to die.

One of the Meanie Butts? Should I have been worried? Even though I'd sensed hate from Adam, I didn't get the feeling that he'd actually do anything about it.

Dad's car swung into the driveway, and I waved at him from the window. I met him in the kitchen.

"Oh good." He put his laptop bag on the kitchen counter. "You made it okay."

"Sorry I forgot to text."

"I'll let Mom know." He pulled out his phone, but it wasn't like she didn't already know from Family Tracker that I was home. Then he glanced outside. "I thought it was clearing up there for a sec, but it's all smoggy again."

I knew it had cleared up as Adam and I walked together. Up until the end. Up until Adam said what he said. And then it was like it hadn't cleared at all.

"Anyway." Dad tore his gaze away from the window. "Mom's working at the clinic until late tonight. Why don't we go to the café for dinner?"

Anything to keep from cooking, right?

Dad pressed a hand to his chest and gave me an exaggerated innocent look. "Who? Me?" He dropped his hand and smiled. "Yes, anything."

Dad and I walked into the Clear Creek Café, and my heart sank when I looked over and saw Valerie sitting at a table with her parents and older sister. My mood worsened even further when I saw they hadn't gotten their food yet.

Valerie looked up at us, and her expression turned mocking. I quickly looked away, careful not to make eye contact with her.

"Hey, you two," Margie said. "You want a table tonight?"

"Table for two," Dad said all cheerily, but any cheer I'd been feeling had gotten squashed by Valerie being in the restaurant. Still, I mustered a weak smile for Dad's sake.

Margie grabbed two plastic menus from behind the counter, and we followed her to a small table by a window. Even though it was on the other side of the restaurant from Valerie, the café was small, too small, and we were the only ones in there. She might as well have been sitting at the table with us.

I sat down and stared out the window at the dirt parking lot. At the dirt in the air. At the dirt-covered cars. Dirt, dirt, dirt.

"You feeling better, honey?" Margie asked.

I turned my head and forced that smile again. "Yes, I'm fine. Thank you."

"That's good to hear. I was worried about you, especially with all this dust we've been having."

Margie left the table, and I stared out the window again, but I could feel Dad's eyes on me. "What was that about?"

"Nothing," I said. "I was having a little asthma attack the other day, so I came in here and got a cup of coffee after school."

Dad seemed to be doing the calculations in his head—my route from school to home didn't bring me by the café. "Why wouldn't you go home if you were having an attack?" Dad asked.

Because mean boys were chasing us.

Because I genuinely feared for my life.

Because I wanted to be where there were other people so I could feel safe.

"I dunno. It was closer than home at the moment, I guess." I braved a glance at Valerie's table and saw that she was watching me while her sister and parents stared at their phones. I looked away.

Margie walked over and set two glasses of ice water on our table with two paper-covered straws. I ordered the only thing on the menu I could: chef salad without croutons or cheese, oil and vinegar on the side. Dad ordered what he always ordered—chicken fried steak. Something we could never have at home.

"Anything happen in school today?" Dad asked.

"Nope."

"But you saw Ms. Imani?"

"Oh yeah. She gave me a breathing treatment."

"She doing okay?"

"Sure." I kept staring out the window, wishing Dad would leave me alone so I could keep a low profile. "She's going to Tahiti this summer."

"Nice. Did you see Dillon and Nan?"

"Of course."

"Did you..." Dad tapped his knuckles on the old wooden table. "Did you have any tests?"

"Nope."

"I heard there's a dance coming up at school."

I turned to him. "Who told you that?"

"Dr. Delgado. I ran into him at the store."

I groaned. Small town. "I'm not going to any dance."

"Why not?"

I grabbed my straw and started pulling the paper down so that it was all scrunched up like an accordion. "I don't even know how to dance, Dad."

"Maybe I could teach you."

Grunting, I carefully slipped the little accordion of paper off my straw.

"A kid was walking away from the house when I pulled in earlier."

I dropped the straw into my ice water. "Huh?"

"That kid wearing black clothes. You know him?"

I pushed my thumb over the top of the straw and pulled it out of my ice water. "Oh...yeah, that was Adam. I told you about him."

"Right. He and his parents just moved here?"

Parents? Adam had said he didn't live with parents. "I really don't know him well at all, Dad. I told you he's quiet." I looked up at Dad. "Why? Have *you* heard anything about his family?"

"No, nothing."

I sighed and held the straw over my little accordion of paper, letting drops fall on it. The paper began unraveling, squirming like a snake. I glanced up at Valerie to see if she was still watching us.

"Cool trick," Dad said.

Once the paper snake stopped squirming, I picked it up and squeezed the water onto the table. "Dillon showed me."

We sat quietly a long time, me ripping my wet straw paper into little pieces and Dad tapping his wedding ring on the corner of the table until he pulled out his phone. "Putrefaction," he read from one of the spelling bee apps.

But I was embarrassed to spell in front of Valerie. Embarrassed to talk to Dad in front of her. Embarrassed to eat in front of her. Embarrassed to just exist in front of her. It felt like my insides were putrefying every second she was nearby.

When Valerie seemed to lose interest, picking up her own phone, I dropped my straw and pushed away from the table. "I have to go to the bathroom."

As I walked by Valerie's table, at all four of them staring at their phones, in their own separate worlds, my annoyance at Dad evaporated.

When I got back to the table, I sat down. "Putrefaction. P-U-T-R-E-F-A-C-T-I-O-N. Putrefaction."

Dad's whole face lit up, and he picked up his phone again. "Equanimity."

"Equanimity," I repeated, forcing myself not to look at Valerie's table. "E-Q-U-A-N-I-M-I-T-Y. Equanimity."

Eventually, as Dad and I spelled more words, I stopped caring about Valerie.

chapter 15

Disquietude.
D-I-S-Q-U-I-E-T-U-D-E.
Disquietude.

I stood in a room. Dust hammered all four walls. Even though the walls were made of glass, I couldn't see outside because the storm had turned the world to a thick, pale fog. I couldn't breathe well either because the room was slowly growing smaller, the walls closing in on me, the oxygen in the room running out.

I woke up gasping for breath. My lungs felt as though someone had tied them into knots so that only a tiny trickle of air could slip through—like when Dad watered the plants outside and the hose got twisted up, turning the stream to a dribble.

Reaching for the inhaler on my nightstand, I sat up and coughed before taking a puff, then coughed some more. I felt as though I were still in the dream, had somehow carried it with me into the real world. Everything was all blurry and suffocating.

Dad showed up with the nebulizer. "Mom's conked out." He set the nebulizer on the bed. "There's a huge drool puddle on her pillow if you want to go check it out when we're done."

My lungs were so tight tonight, I could barely force a smile. "Sure," I muttered.

"Double shift." He yawned and handed me the mouthpiece. "She needs some sleep." He stared down at me as he turned on the machine. "You okay?"

I nodded and breathed in the medication.

"This has been a lot, with all these dust storms. I think I'll call the doctor in the morning. If I can get you in, we'll keep you home tomorrow."

A day off school sounded amazing. I gave him a thumbs-up.

"I'll stay home, too." He rubbed my head, knocking my hair into my face. "Just you and me, kid, playing hooky."

Pushing my hair away from my eyes with my free

hand, I smiled. Steam poured out around my mouth, so I quickly clamped my lips back down around the mouthpiece.

"Let me know if you need me."

I gave him another thumbs-up.

"Don't forget to come check out the drool," he mumbled on his way out, sounding like he was falling back to sleep on his feet.

As my lungs opened and the sounds of dust faded from a loud rumble to a gentle whisper, the memory of the room of glass melted away, too. Until the next morning.

Mom, Dad, and I stood outside after the sun had risen, staring at the south wall of the house. The best word I could think of to describe their faces was disquietude. D-I-S-Q-U-I-E-T-U-D-E. Disquietude. Like how I'd felt during my dream. And after.

Mom pointed at the wall. "The paint is wearing off."

Dad rubbed his chin, his face filled with disquietude, then ran a hand over the bare spots on the wall. "It's like someone used a sandblaster on it."

"What's a sandblaster?" I asked.

"A tool that blasts sand," Dad said.

"Great explanation, professor." Mom rolled her eyes. "It's a tool that blows sand out of a nozzle to clean off old paint and rust and stuff." She pointed at the bare spot on the house. "Just like that." The dust always seemed to blow in the same direction lately—from the south northward. My room was on the south side of the house, so that was why it was extra loud in my room during storms.

Mom took the corner of her cardigan and rubbed at my window. "Huh. I'll need to get some heavy-duty cleaner."

I ran my fingertip across the smear she'd made, but the blotches didn't go away. Like they'd been painted on. Or sandblasted.

Dad had already taken the day off of work so he could take me to the doctor. He was usually the one to miss work for me because Mom was an orthopedic nurse and Dad sold software for a small business, so it was a lot easier for Dad to do his work from home in our guest room, which doubled as an office and storage space. There were still boxes stacked in there that hadn't been opened since we moved here ten years ago.

I loved it when Dad stayed home with me because that meant a *real* day off from school. I ate blueberries and watched *Akeelah and the Bee* while he worked until it was time to leave.

The doctor visit that afternoon was brief. Dr. Abrams told me to start using my peak flow meter—the little device I blew into that basically told me how open my lungs were—twice a day. I was to keep a strict record of my numbers and then we would meet again in a couple of weeks to see how things were going. I wasn't sure if Dad even knew where my peak flow meter was; I hadn't had to use it in a really long time.

"I'm sure things will be better in a couple of weeks anyway," Dad said in the car on the way home. "I mean, this dust can't last forever, right?"

I wasn't so sure. I was starting to get the feeling it would last as long as Adam stayed in town.

chapter 16

Surveillance.
S-U-R-V-E-I-L-L-A-N-C-E.
Surveillance.

I couldn't stop thinking about Adam. About all the dust storms. About the haze in the air and how it seemed to always be worse when Adam was in a bad mood. About the day with the dust devil when Bryden stole my inhaler.

I really wanted to know where Adam lived, to see if that could give me any clues about who he was. Who he lived with. Some clues as to why he was so lonely. And why he was so...whatever that awful dungeon feeling was. Since he wouldn't let me come to his house, I knew this would include some, well, spying. But just a little. And not for any nefarious purposes.

I barely said goodbye to Nan and Dillon when the bell rang after language arts. I had to hurry, taking a different route from my normal one so as not to run into Adam. How could I secretly follow him if he saw me after school? So I walked quickly down a trail through the desert, getting a bunch of cactus needles stuck in the soles of my tennis shoes. Despite the poking pain in the bottom of my feet, I kept going.

I got home and sat in the living room, facing the window that looked onto the road. While I waited, I took off my shoes and tried picking the needles out. Then I texted with Dillon and Nan in our group chat about the giant booger sticking out of Mr. Cumberland's nose today. It had been there during both of our periods, which meant it was there a *long* time.

It was also taking a long time for Adam to walk by. I didn't understand how I could've possibly missed him. Maybe he was staying after school with Ms. Lund. I didn't want to sit here all day waiting for him.

He finally appeared, and I put my phone down,

my heart pounding with excitement. Now the espionage could begin. E-S-P-I-O-N-A-G-E. Espionage.

As he walked by, he glanced at my house. Was he wondering if I was home? But he kept walking.

Creeping into my side yard, I hid behind our large mesquite tree and peeked out to watch him until he was about a block away. When he turned a corner, I left to follow him. Luckily, a broken-down truck for sale stood on the corner, and I hid behind it, glancing back at the imprinted letters my shoes had left behind in the dirt: *S, U, R, V, E, I, L, L, A, N, C, E.*

When Adam turned another corner, I followed him, reaching the next corner right as he walked up the driveway of a house and disappeared inside.

It was a completely normal-looking house: adobe-style like so many in the area, a few cactuses in the front, an old shed near the side. It was just totally... normal.

I guess I'd expected a run-down shack or a bunch of garbage and broken-down vehicles in the front or something—anything that would explain why Adam didn't want me to come over. It couldn't be that he really wasn't allowed to have friends over. I'd never

even heard of such a thing. I'd figured he was probably poor and embarrassed about it.

But nothing about Adam's house could explain
anything to me. I turned around and walked home,
more confused than ever about who he really was.

chapter 17

Conductivity.
C-O-N-D-U-C-T-I-V-I-T-Y.
Conductivity.

Dillon sat cross-legged on our fake grass, the hose in his lap. "So I just want you guys to know"—he took a deep breath—"I'm going to that dance. With or without you." He lifted the spray nozzle and pulled the trigger, showering us with cold water.

Mom and Dad had put the small rectangle of grass in our backyard a few years ago. We had fake grass instead of real grass for a few reasons. One, it was really hard to keep real grass alive in the desert, and it took a ton of watering. Two, Dad didn't like to mow a lawn and said he definitely wasn't going to spend "his whole life" caring for a small patch of grass. And three, I was allergic to real grass. Of course.

It had been difficult to keep the grass clean with all the dust storms, though. Mom was constantly raking and sweeping and brushing it off. I'd even seen her out here one day with a long extension cord and the vacuum cleaner.

Nan and I wiped our faces. "What? Why are you doing this?" she asked. "You want to spend *more* time with the Meanie Butt Band?"

"Why shouldn't we go? Why should we be the ones to stay home?"

I shook my head. "Nope."

"Double nope," Nan added.

"Triple yep." Dillon squinted at us in the bright sun. "I'm going. I'm not going to let them ruin my whole year."

"Go ahead and go," Nan said. "Have fun with that."

Dillon's face sagged, and it was hard to tell if he was turning red about the dance or from the sun. Dillon's face always got red in the sun, even though

I'd watched him slather on a pound of sunscreen. "You'd really make me go by myself?"

My mouth dropped open. "You'd really make us go with you?"

Dillon looked like he might cry. I needed to change the subject. Grabbing the hose from him, I fell back onto the grass and held the spray nozzle up high above me, pointed toward the sky. "Let's talk about telekinesis again, please?" I pressed the trigger and a geyser exploded into the air, showering us and the grass with its cool mist. It was only in the 80s, but one downside of the fake grass was that it got blazing hot even in mild weather

Nan let out a dramatic sigh. "Not more X-Men stuff." She stretched out on the grass like a starfish in her purple-striped bathing suit. She'd moved up to wearing bikinis, but I was still in my old blue one-piece.

"No." I released the trigger and watched the mist evaporate in the air. "I thought of some new questions."

Dillon wiped the water from his face. "Like what?"

"Like…" I put the hose down and rolled onto my stomach, the grass warming my whole middle.

I pushed myself up on my elbows. "Okay, so if it's possible to send electrical brain signals, do you think someone's brain could make enough electricity to move something?"

"I already told you no," said Dillon. "It's not possible."

"But..." I pulled on a wet, fake plastic blade of grass, which stretched thin before snapping. I sat up. "Have you ever noticed that when we're about to get a dust storm, you can feel it coming? You can feel the static electricity in the air." I twirled the little green sliver in my fingers.

"Yeah," said Dillon. "That's probably from dryness."

"No, I looked it up." I couldn't believe I knew a scientific fact that Dillon didn't. I tried not to act too arrogant about it. "It's from all the grains of sand bouncing around and hitting one another."

"Interesting." Dillon yawned. He grabbed the hose and pointed it at me, one eye squinted shut.

"Or maybe...it could be coming from someone's mind?" I said to him.

"No." He unleashed the water at my face, and I put my hand up to block the attack.

Nan's face twisted up in disbelief. "Are you serious, Avalyn?"

I pushed my wet hair back and wiped my eyes. "I'm just speaking theoretically. I'm not saying *I* think the dust storms are caused by someone's mind." I snorted before looking at Dillon. "But... could they be?"

"Avalyn, come on. You can't move things with your mind," Dillon said to me in full know-it-all mode, as though I were four years old and having trouble understanding. I could see why he got on some people's nerves. "You just can't." He sprayed me again.

I snatched the hose from him. "But you said people are moving things with their minds now with computers."

"It's all about conductivity. You can't move things without a conductor."

I resisted the urge to spray him in the face. "Conductivity." I rolled the word around on my tongue. "C-O-N-D-U-C-T-I-V-I-T-Y."

"Right. Conductivity."

"What about something that can conduct but is

also really, really tiny? Like the grains of sand? Or what if it has something to do with what's in the sand? What's our sand made of?"

Dillon rolled over and crawled lazily across the fake grass on hands and knees until he reached the raw desert ground. He scooped up a handful of dirt and inspected it. "Probably quartz and other rock."

"What about metal?" I asked. "You said metal is a good conductor."

He tilted his hand around at different angles, making the sand glitter in the sun. "There's definitely some iron pyrite."

"Oh, I know what that is." Nan raised her hand as if we were in class. "Fool's gold."

"Could be a little copper," said Dillon. "A little silver. All the things people have mined from here. Maybe even tiny flakes of real gold. But it's mostly rock."

I squeezed the hose tightly in my hands. Metal control. Rock control. I couldn't figure it out. "It just seems like someone out there might be able to move a single grain of sand with their mind."

Dillon opened his mouth wide in pretend

excitement. "Or maybe the fossils in our rock could somehow be controlled. Maybe even brought back to life."

Oh, fossils. I hadn't thought of that. But I stuck my tongue out at him. "Don't make fun of me."

"Sorry. Okay, for real, though." Dillon stared at the dirt in his hand, his hazel eyes focused and serious. Finally, he shook his head. "Nope. Nothing's moving."

Nan crawled across the grass as Dillon had. "Let me try." She stared intently at his palms. "Still not moving, Avalyn."

"What about wind?" I said. "Could someone move the wind?" I remembered the air I'd felt from Adam—how it had seemed like it had blown me up to bursting.

Dillon threw the dirt back onto the ground. "You can't move anything with your mind. Unless you have some kind of computer to connect your mind to the object, it's just not possible." He held his dirt-smeared hands up for me, and I sprayed them clean with the hose.

Nan leaned into the stream so the water would

hit her head. Then she shook out her dark hair. "Can we please talk about something else? People can't read minds or send messages with their minds or move things with their minds. All our minds do is think about stuff."

But I was pretty sure they could do a lot more than that.

chapter 18

Euphemism.
E-U-P-H-E-M-I-S-M.
Euphemism.

I watched out my window the following morning, waiting for Adam to walk by. When I spotted him, I opened my front door and called out, "Hey!"

He stopped and turned, standing in the middle of the dirt road. "Hey," he said softly.

As soon as I reached him, I blurted out, "So I thought of a way spelling could be a superpower."

We continued walking together. "Okay…"

"Okay. So let's say some villain has stolen all the world's frogs, and—"

Adam snorted. "Why would that matter?"

"Are you kidding me?" I cried. "It would set off a terrible chain reaction that would eventually destroy everything. Anyway, as I was saying—this villain has stolen all the world's frogs and is speaking over some machine that everyone in the whole world can hear, and he's like," I deepened my voice and did my best British accent, which didn't sound British at all—"'I shall only release the frogs if there is anyone out there who can spell the word... *esquamulose*.'"

The corner of Adam's mouth tipped upward a little. "Then what happens?"

"Then I'm all like, 'Me! That's me! Esquamulose. E-S-Q-U-A-M-U-L-O-S-E. Esquamulose.' Then he releases all the frogs, and boom! Spelling saved the day."

"What's *esquamulose*?"

"It means smooth. No scales. Like a frog's skin."

"So what *would* happen if all the frogs were gone?"

"All the animals that eat frogs would die, and the insects frogs used to eat would take over the world!"

Adam laughed softly, and it was such a nice sound I couldn't help laughing with him. "That would be terrible." He side-eyed me. "But I still don't think spelling can be a superpower."

I gave him a mean look. "You're wrong, and I'll prove you wrong."

We'd reached school, but before he could break away from me, I said, "Dillon's making us go to that dance. Do you think you'll go?"

Adam's eyes darted to a poster on the wall and then back to me. "I don't know. Ms. Lund wants me to take pictures."

"Then you should go. You can come with us if you want. I mean with me and Dillon and Nan."

"I don't know." Then he gave me a little wave and hurried away. It was like once we hit school property, he couldn't bear to speak anymore. He just hid inside himself.

I turned to look at the poster Adam had noticed, wondering who'd put it up. Probably Dr. Delgado. Ever since he got to our school this year, he'd been trying to make all kinds of changes, like doing the morning announcements himself and the dance and now these posters. But Dr. Delgado was only one person, and the problems at CCC Middle School were way bigger than one person could ever solve.

ZERO TOLERANCE FOR BULLYING, the poster read in big, bold, red letters.

I continued walking, reading the headlines of the rest of the posters plastered on the cinder-block walls.

BULLYING PREVENTION TIPS.

DON'T BE A BULLY.

Someone actually shouted "Wheezer" at me while I was walking by a poster that read, NAME CALLING IS BULLYING.

I walked around school, reading the posters and muttering the word "bully" over and over again under my breath until it lost all meaning and just began to sound like noise. Because that's really what had happened with that word. We talked about bullying so much that the word had lost all power. It had become nothing more than a euphemism. E-U-P-H-E-M-I-S-M. Euphemism.

Other words for bully: *harass, abuse, assault, hurt.*

Maybe those were the words we should have been using instead. Maybe if we used those words, everyone would take the bullying more seriously than they did with these stupid, pointless posters. I wanted to rip them off the walls and tear them into a million pieces. I stood in front of one that read, DON'T BE MEAN BEHIND YOUR SCREEN, which had a picture of a phone and was about cyberbullying.

That was one way they couldn't bully me. It was bad enough dealing with it at school, but then to go home and deal with it? No, thank you. I'd been on social media for about two weeks after starting middle school before I left and never went back.

I made the mistake of posting about the Super Spellers and then tagging a bunch of people I didn't realize had suddenly decided to hate me somewhere between elementary and middle school. I still didn't know who LetterLoser and SpellingBeesSuck and AvalynIsANerd were, but those trolls showed up and made me cry. And made me throw my spelling book into the garbage. Dad had dug it out and wiped all the potato peels and margarine off it.

I was about to give in to my urge to tear the cyberbullying poster off the wall when Nan suddenly jumped in front of me. "Hello, marvelous person."

I didn't feel all that marvelous at the moment, but I managed to utter back, "Hello, marvelous person."

"You okay?" she asked. "You look mad."

I walked along the sidewalk with her, leaving the poster behind. "I am mad, Nan. I'm very mad."

"At that poster you were glaring at?"

"Yes, at the poster. And the jerks who ruined social media for me."

Nan nodded understandably. "The Super Spellers would've been epic."

"I know!" I shouted, and we giggled, my anger starting to dissolve. "I wish I could go back to when I was a blissfully ignorant fifth grader."

"Remember how Emma actually used to be nice? She came to your tenth birthday party."

"Oh yeah." I even remembered the gift she'd brought me—a big eye-shadow kit when I wasn't allowed to wear eye shadow yet. I should've known right then we were going in very different directions. "What happened exactly?"

Nan thought for a moment and then nodded wisely as if she'd figured it all out. "Toxic environment."

"That explains everything."

"And, you know... Dillon."

"Dillon," I repeated.

Nan stood up straighter and jutted out her chin. "No one can tell us who we can or can't be friends with."

"Right," I agreed quickly.

As though we'd somehow made them appear, the Meanie Butts were walking toward us. We didn't even have to think about it—our moving out of their way was automatic. Apparently they still felt we were taking up too much space because Caleb deliberately bumped me as they walked by, squishing me against the wall. "Watch it, Wheezer!" he ordered, and Valerie and Emma laughed. But Caleb must've seen something in my face, something surprising, because he faltered in his meanness for a second. "What?" he demanded.

I shook my head. "Nothing."

Caleb kept looking at me as he walked away. Maybe what he'd seen in my eyes was the realization that he was a fake. A fraud. Because when Caleb had bumped me, it felt like my chest tore open and let some of my insides out, leaving me all empty and prickly inside.

Caleb was surrounded by friends. But he felt completely alone. And scared. He was just as scared as we were—scared of messing up. Scared of being kicked out. Scared of doing anything that might make him a target.

I tried to send him a message with my face. *You're a pretender, Caleb.*

He quickly turned away, and Nan breathed out. "Thank goodness, they're gone."

But I was still watching Caleb's back. At one point, when they were far away, he glanced back again, his face full of fear, as if someone had figured him out. I had.

Nan grabbed my shoulder. "Forget about them."

I turned to her. "Yeah, forget about them."

"So my mom offered to take us into town after school if you want to go buy a new outfit for the dance."

"Ugh," I said. "Don't remind me. Why is Dillon making us go again?"

"He seems determined lately to not let the Meanie Butt Band get to him."

I snickered because *Meanie Butt Band* was never *not* funny.

But this dance would definitely be not funny. And also not fun. For whatever reason, though, Dillon was set on going, and we promised him we would, too. When it came down to it, Nan and I couldn't let him go alone.

"He's been acting so weird lately, don't you think?" said Nan. "First, he stood up to Bryden in language arts when he called you Wheezer."

"Which got him a bloody cheek," I added.

"Then, when Bryden and Caleb called him a girl the other day, he smiled sweetly and pretended to put lipstick on. Then he walked away all shaking his hips and—get this—turned around and blew them a kiss." Her eyes were huge.

I stopped. "When did all this happen?"

"I think you were at home sick."

"How did they react?" I asked.

"They glared at him with this *You're totally going to get it now* look."

"I know that look." It made me feel scared for Dillon.

"Then Emma walked by and shouted at me, 'Vete a freír espárragos!' and Dillon told her that her Mexican accent was terrible, which it is of course, and that she probably didn't even know what she said, even though I'm pretty sure Dillon doesn't know what it means either. But he could probably just tell by the way she said it that it was something bad. And also because she's Emma."

Even though Nan's family had moved here from

Mexico a long time ago, before Nan was even born, the Meanie Butts still called her *illegal* and constantly tried to say mean things in Spanish to her. "What does it mean?" I asked.

"Well, what it literally means is 'go fry an asparagus.' But what it *really* means is…" She made a rude gesture with her hand.

"Um, okay."

"Anyway," Nan continued, getting all worked up at the memory, "Emma said she was so sorry she couldn't speak perfect Mexican, and Dillon said Mexican isn't even a language, and if Emma knew anything at all, she would at least know that." Nan snickered. "That kind of made me laugh. But then he got another *I'm going to get you for that* look."

"Wow," I said. "He shouldn't antagonize them like that."

Nan gritted her teeth. "They deserve it."

I nodded. "So, like, I still don't get the whole asparagus thing. I mean, why—"

"It's just stupid and pointless," Nan blurted. "People *boil* asparagus and *roast* asparagus and *grill* asparagus and, who knows, they probably even eat it, like, raw. But no one *fries* asparagus."

I nodded like I got it. But I still really didn't. "Okay..."

"Two years of dealing with their garbage," Nan said. "I can't wait until summer."

"Me too." I just hoped Dillon made it that long.

chapter 19

Zephyr.
Z-E-P-H-Y-R.
Zephyr.

The thought of spending even one millisecond at that dance alone was horrifying, so Dillon and Nan came over to my house so we could all show up together. I knew exactly how the rest of it would all go down: (1) find a quiet spot in a corner where no one would notice us, (2) do not do any dancing whatsoever, (3) quietly creep out the moment the dance ends.

I heard a knock on the door and opened it. Dillon stood there, looking amazing in his new pair of flowery Vans and a button-down shirt with sunglass-wearing pineapples all over it. He looked me over. "Hello, marvelous person."

"Hello, marvelous person," I said back.

"I like that new dress."

"Nan and I picked it out together." I curtsied (or did what I thought a curtsy looked like) and let him in. "Target had a buy one dress, get one half-off sale, so Nan got one, too."

Dillon blinked at me. "Matching dresses, huh?" He covered his smile with his hand.

I smacked his arm. "She didn't buy the same exact dress, dork."

Once Nan showed up, Mom and Dad made us stand in the yard together in front of our giant ocotillo so they could take a million pictures of us. "Going to a dance for the very first time," Dad said excitedly. "Are you all up-to-date on the coolest dance moves?"

Dillon gave him a wary look. "Like what?"

"You know, the Running Man. The Roger Rabbit. The Sprinkler." Dad proceeded to put one hand behind his ear and stretch his other arm out—and do the Sprinkler for us. I gave him my best look of disgust while Nan and Dillon giggled.

"You're a terrible dancer," Mom said, still snapping pictures of us, even though we were staring at Dad instead of the camera. "Terrible."

"You're just jealous of my moves." Then Dad shouted out, "Hammer time!" and began moving side-to-side like a really fast crab, kicking up gravel everywhere.

"Please stop embarrassing yourself," Mom said.

Everyone was laughing as I gazed at the distant sunset, which was turning the sky pink and orange. The air was cool and clear, and I hoped it would stay that way tonight.

We did exactly as I expected—we were able to find a dark table in a corner, where we immediately sat and did our best to go unnoticed. Dillon looked from me to Nan and back to me. "I'm going to force one of you to dance with me before this is over."

"Avalyn volunteers," said Nan.

"No way am I dancing." I stared at the group out on the floor as they moved into some kind of conga line, apparently having the time of their lives. Then they formed a dancing circle. The Meanie Butts were very selective about those they let into the circle, and everyone else who wasn't invited was keeping their distance like us.

I felt totally disgusted. Disgusted with the circle of people for acting all happy when there were so many of us who were miserable. But I also felt disgusted with myself. Because deep down, I wanted to be a part of that happy, dancing circle. So badly.

Dr. Delgado stopped by our table. "Hey, you three." He looked like he'd gotten dressed up for the occasion. He always wore button-down shirts and slacks at school, but tonight he wore a full suit with a blue tie and everything.

"Hi, Dr. Delgado," I said.

He put his hands on his hips. "Why aren't you dancing with the rest of them?"

"We're not big dancers," said Nan.

"You can't go to a dance without dancing," Dr. Delgado said.

"Just watch us," Nan mumbled.

I felt bad for Dr. Delgado. I could tell he was trying, and he really did seem to care about his students, but cheerful morning announcements, some posters, and a dance weren't enough. He probably thought a dance would bring everyone together, but it just made us feel more like outcasts.

Dr. Delgado stared down at us. "Well, if I go out there and dance, then you three have to dance, too."

I thought of Dad and assumed Dr. Delgado's dancing wouldn't be much different.

"Deal," said Dillon.

"Great," said Dr. Delgado. "I'll see you out there, then."

"No, you will not," Nan muttered as he walked away.

Two songs played while the three of us sat at our table, watching the dance floor from our dark corner. "This is so stupid," said Dillon. "Did we seriously come here to not even dance?"

Nan gaped at him. "Yes, that's exactly what we did."

"You forced us to come," I added. "Did you forget we didn't want to dance?"

Dillon crossed his arms and pouted. "Fine."

"Look," said Nan. "There's your archnemesis, Avalyn."

I scanned the cafeteria and spotted Daniel Garza with a couple of his friends, huddling in a corner like us and almost everyone except the Meanie Butt Band and the few people they'd decided they didn't hate for the time being. When Daniel saw me watching him, I waved and he waved back. Then he got up from his table and started moving toward us.

Nan laughed. "Uh-oh. Here he comes."

We were just joking about Daniel. Even though he'd beaten me at the spelling bee last year, we all liked him. When he reached our table, he lifted his fists up as if we were about to get into an actual fight. "You ready for the spelling bee, Avalyn?"

"Totally," I said. "Prepare to be annihilated. A-N-N-I-H-I-L-A-T-E-D."

Daniel smirked. "You prepare to be extirpated. E-X-T-I-R-P-A-T-E-D."

"Prepare to be pulverized," I countered. "P-U-L-V-E-R-I-Z-E-D."

Nan groaned. "This is the nerdiest conversation I've ever heard."

Daniel and I punched the air at each other, and then he smiled and waved awkwardly at the three of us before running back to his own table, where he and his friends stayed hunched and wary, periodically glancing at the Meanie Butt Band.

Nan said, "It is good to know there's at least one person who's a bigger dork than we are out there."

I kept scanning the room and saw someone standing at the snack table, holding up a camera looped around his neck. He snapped a picture of the table and lowered the camera. It took me a minute to realize who it was—Adam. He wasn't wearing his usual black. Instead, he had on jeans and what appeared to be a light blue T-shirt. He'd combed back his overgrown hair so it wasn't falling into his eyes.

"Well, look who took a shower and changed his clothes," said Nan.

I clucked my tongue. "That's mean, Nan."

I watched Adam as he spotted us from across the cafeteria and began moving in our direction, his head down, the camera held firmly in his hands. He skirted as widely as possible around the dancing crowd, but he still didn't manage to escape their notice. Valerie and Emma stopped dancing and watched him walk by, their mouths hanging open, as though they couldn't possibly believe he would dare show up here. My heart pounded, and a sick feeling built in my stomach as they ran over to Bryden and Caleb.

Adam stopped in front of our table. His mouth moved, but the music drowned out his quiet voice.

"What?" hollered Dillon.

"I'm here to take pictures for Ms. Lund," he said more loudly this time. "For the yearbook." Then he stood there awkwardly, and I realized we only had three chairs at our little table. We all glanced at one another while Adam fidgeted with his camera. The silence between us made me shift in my seat, wishing someone would say something.

I looked across the cafeteria and saw Emma, Valerie, Bryden, and Caleb all gathered together in a tight group, heads together. Then the four of them snuck outside through the cafeteria doors. They weren't dancing. They weren't dirty-looking anyone. They were gone. I had no idea why they'd left, and I didn't care. All I felt was relief at their disappearance. So much relief that I took a chance and jumped up from my seat, knocking my chair over. "Do you want to dance?"

Adam stopped his fidgeting and stared at me. My heart pounded. I glanced at Nan and Dillon. They were looking at me like I'd just started tap dancing in the middle of the dance floor. I looked back at Adam. "Well...do you?"

"Okay," Adam said softly.

Suddenly the seriousness of what I asked hit me, especially as a slow song came on. Dancing meant touching. For like five minutes if we made it through one song. What if Adam felt like the dungeon? Could I handle it for five minutes? Maybe this would be a good opportunity to test if I was really feeling it from him and not making it up in my mind like the letters I saw in everything.

When Adam and I got to the dance floor, I tried to relax and clear my mind. I'd never slow danced with a boy before, so I did what I'd seen the other kids do while we'd spent all that time watching from our dark corner—I faced him and put my shaking hands on his shoulders, bracing myself for what I might feel.

His nervousness added to mine, and I sensed that dark dungeon feeling somewhere deep inside, like a distant, awful echo. Not only had Adam closed a door on it and put one of those secret bookcase entrances over it, but he'd now filled the shelves to bursting with heavy, thick books so that no could enter and discover the secrets hidden inside. Maybe not even him.

I forced myself to shift my weight from foot to foot, sort of swaying, but Adam stood there like a statue. I stopped and dropped my hands from his shoulders. Then I grabbed his hands and put them on my waist. "I think you're supposed to do this." My stomach suddenly cramped and twisted like the time I went on this parachute ride at the Arizona State Fair. Pain shot through my arms and legs. My face flushed. Was this how Adam felt? Or was it was just me? "And move like this." I forced myself to put my hands back on his shoulders and swayed from foot to foot again.

Adam stared at me, but still he didn't move. If I was feeling even a tiny fraction of what he was feeling, then I could understand why he was frozen.

I stopped and dropped my hands from his shoulders. I guess he took that as an invitation to remove his own hands from my waist. My emotions began calming as soon as our contact broke. The pain in my limbs eased. My face cooled. My heart slowed its pounding. "We don't have to do this."

He nodded just slightly.

"Let's go back to the table," I said. "I'll find another chair."

He nodded more enthusiastically now. We walked back to the table, and I left the three of them there while I went to find a folding chair. I mean, it was okay that Adam didn't want to dance with me. And it wasn't like I'd felt any kind of disgust coming from him. Like, he didn't seem grossed out by me or anything. So at least there was that.

I had to walk over to the snack table to find a chair, and on my way back, I saw that the Meanie Butt Band was in the cafeteria again. Bryden carried a paper bowl in both hands as though he were worried about spilling whatever was in it. The four of them moved toward our table, snickering and making faces at one another.

I made my way quickly back to my friends, watching the Meanie Butts the whole time as they wove through the dancing kids. Nan and Dillon were talking to Adam, and none of them saw Bryden coming toward them with the paper bowl until he had it held right over Adam's head.

But I'd seen it coming, and for once I didn't think it through—I just acted. I dropped the folding chair and leaped the last few feet to reach them. I slapped Bryden's arm up, and the contents of the bowl burst into the air in a giant brown cloud. Then dirt showered down on everyone, including Valerie and Emma, who were standing behind Bryden. They went from smirking to shrieking, their hands raised and splayed. Their trendy, probably expensive, dresses were all dusted in brown.

Adam jumped up from the table, knocking his chair down. He whirled around, stirring the cloudy air. I inhaled a swirling wisp of it, and my lungs instantly tightened.

"What the—?" Nan pushed back in her chair and threw a hand across Dillon in a protective way, like Mom did to me in the car when she had to slam on the brakes, as if my seatbelt were no match for her arm muscles. Nan's first thought was probably that they were going after Dillon.

Valerie shook her long dark hair out, and dirt flew around her head, adding to the cloudiness in the cafeteria air. She made a noise that sounded like "Gah!"

Bryden crumpled the paper bowl in his hands and threw it at me, where it bounced off my aching chest. "I'm going to kill you for that," he said through gritted teeth. Some people would have taken that as an empty threat, but I remembered how he and Caleb had stolen my inhaler, and knew the threat was definitely not empty.

"What's going on over here?" a deep voice bellowed, and I turned to find Dr. Delgado moving toward us.

While the Meanie Butt Band was distracted, I grabbed Adam's hand and we snuck toward the doors. I barely had time to glance back at Nan and Dillon before we pushed out onto the dark campus.

Adam's adrenaline combined with mine, making the excitement inside me multiply. It felt like the mouse running around inside my chest had grown into a rhinoceros as we ran around the cafeteria building, looking for anywhere to hide. We reached the back delivery driveway and crouched next to a stack of milk crates. We didn't speak. We just listened.

After a while, we heard slapping footsteps. Then voices.

"Where did they go?" asked Caleb.

"She's so dead," said Bryden.

I desperately wanted a puff of my inhaler, but I kept quiet next to Adam, doing my best to take slow, deep breaths.

At one point, the boys got so close that I swore I could smell the potato chips on their nasty breath.

"Come out, come out, wherever you are," said Bryden.

"Man, let's just go back to the dance," said Caleb. "Forget about those dweebs."

Caleb moved closer to me, and I covered my mouth with my hands, as though I could hide my wheezing. I felt like I was on the verge of suffocating. And then Caleb turned around, backing up so he was next to the milk crates, between us and Bryden. Was he...hiding us?

"I heard a noise!" Caleb cried. "Out there in the desert!"

"Let's go!" said Bryden.

When the footsteps started moving away, I fumbled into my dress pocket with shaking hands and pulled out my inhaler, taking a puff and breathing it in as quietly as I could, holding it in as long as possible.

"Are you okay?" Adam whispered.

I breathed out. "Yeah, you?"

He nodded. My legs began cramping from squatting, so I leaned back against the rough cinder-block wall and sat down, my knees pulled up to my chest. Adam pointed at me. "You got some dirt on your dress."

I looked down at the light brown smear over my new Target dress. "I don't even care. That felt so good."

"What?"

"That." I touched the smear. "Just…doing something." I thought about what might have happened if I'd just watched them—watched them pour that dirt on Adam's head. I'd finally done something, and despite the boys chasing us down, despite my sudden asthma attack, despite the dirt on my new dress, I felt like I could do anything. "I couldn't stand to watch them pour that dirt on you."

I looked him up and down. He didn't have a speck on him. That had been a pretty big cloud, and some had even gotten on me. But he looked completely untouched. Then my eyes landed on his face, which looked stunned. "Oh," he said softly. His throat moved like he was swallowing a lot. "Thank you, then."

"I'll never forget the looks on Emma's and Valerie's faces as long as I live." I pressed my face into my hands and laughed softly. Then I peeked at Adam through splayed fingers.

He smiled. "Yeah, that was good."

Adam finally seemed to relax enough to sit down. As he leaned back against the wall, his arm brushed mine. I felt something from him I'd never gotten before. It was just a tiny drop of it. Or maybe I should say...a tiny spark of it.

On Fourth of July, Mom, Dad, and I always lit sparklers together outside. It was too dry in the desert to light full-blown fireworks, but sparklers were okay.

And I loved our sparklers.

We would run around the yard, swirling them in our outstretched arms, hold them up to the stars, and write words made of light, challenging one another to guess what they were. Sometimes Dad would write words like *barf* and *fart* to get a reaction out of Mom, and she would pretend to be offended as he hoped she would. Fireworks probably would've been pretty cool, but sparklers were more than enough for us.

That feeling coming from Adam was like one of those sparklers had lit inside of me. It exploded in a burst of light and was writing letters in the dark: *Z, E, P, H, Y, R.*

I looked up at the night sky, at the stars shining

more brightly than I'd seen in weeks. Maybe this was the moment I could finally figure all this out. "You never did say why you moved here."

He looked up at the stars. "My grandma had a stroke," he finally said. "She couldn't take care of me anymore."

"I'm sorry. Did you live with her here in Arizona?"

"No, in Seattle."

"Did you always live with her?"

He shook his head, still looking up at the sky. "No, I lived with my mom."

"Where's your mom now?"

His face darkened, and I could tell just by looking at him that the sparkler I'd sensed a minute ago had gotten totally snuffed out. "She's dead."

"Oh…" I didn't know what to say to something like that. I'd never known someone whose parents had died. "How—"

"I don't want to talk about it."

We sat there quietly awhile. Finally, I said, "Is it okay if I just ask when she died?"

He turned his head, his eyebrows drawn together. "Why?"

I thought about Mom and Dad, and what it

would feel like if one of them died. Was that what Adam carried around with him in that dungeon? I couldn't even begin to imagine the sadness I would feel, but would it feel like *that*? It still didn't seem to make sense. "I don't know. I think if my mom died… I don't know if I could ever stop feeling sad. That must've been really horrible for you."

He didn't answer, and I pushed my head back against the cinder-block wall. We listened to an owl hooting somewhere. Crickets chirping. The distant sound of the cafeteria doors opening and closing as people went in and out. I wondered when it would be safe to go back to the dance. Probably never. I hoped the Meanie Butts weren't taking out their anger on Nan and Dillon.

"She died a year ago," Adam suddenly said. Then he added in a whisper, "A year ago, tomorrow."

"Oh…so you always lived in Seattle, then?"

"No, I was born here in Phoenix."

"You were? Why'd you move away?"

"My mom said the whole time she was in the hospital having me, there was a horrible dust storm outside. She said it was so bad, it made it look like nighttime even during the day, and ambulances couldn't get around town. Plus, there were tons of accidents, so the whole city was in chaos. We left Arizona right after I was born."

Wow. It was the most he'd ever told me at once. "Why?"

He swallowed and looked back up at the speckled sky. "She said she couldn't stand the dust, so she moved us to the wettest place she could think of—a place too wet for dust."

"Seattle," I said.

"Seattle."

I wanted to ask him more questions, but I worried if I pressured him too much, he would shut me out again. I had a lot to think about, especially what his mom had said—that she couldn't stand the dust. But I assumed she'd lived in Arizona before Adam was born. So the dust only became too much for her after he was born? So much so that she felt the need to move somewhere too wet for dust?

Adam had opened up to me for once, and that was big progress. I decided to let all my other burning questions go for tonight. The air was cool with the slightest breeze. The sky was crystal clear as Adam and I hid behind the cafeteria together.

As soon as I got home from the dance, I went to my computer and searched for Seattle news stories on the date of Adam's mom's death. I didn't find any mention of a woman's death. But Seattle had had an unusually bad windstorm that day—so bad it knocked down trees and power lines and blew people's shingles right off their roofs.

But just as Adam's mom said—Seattle was too wet for dust.

chapter 20

Solicitation.
S-O-L-I-C-I-T-A-T-I-O-N.
Solicitation.

The air was absolutely terrible the next day.

Luckily it was a Sunday, so I didn't have to worry about missing school. But I couldn't stop thinking about Adam and what was going on with him. It was the anniversary of his mom's death. The air was so awful, though, could something else be going on with him? Or was it only that? Or was I seriously losing it thinking all these things? I wished I could call him, but he didn't have a cell phone, and I didn't have a clue how to go about finding his home phone number.

Who did he live with?

Mom, Dad, and I sat at breakfast as we usually did on Sunday mornings. They wanted to know all about the dance, but I didn't know what to tell them. Last night, I'd been feeling all great about what I'd done, knocking the bowl of dirt out of Bryden's hands, but it must have been the adrenaline or something because now I felt an awful sense of impending doom—like I was in that room, the one made of glass walls, and the walls were closing in and the dust was growing worse and breathing was getting harder and harder in the tiny space. My stomach got sicker with every second closer to going back to school, and I found myself wishing the dust would stay bad so I could stay home.

"The dance was fine."

"Just fine?" said Mom. "Did you do any dancing?"

"A little." I thought of my minute on the dance floor with Adam.

"Did you dance with any boys?" Dad waggled his eyebrows at me.

"No," I lied. Well, sort of lied. I would hardly call what Adam and I did dancing.

"What about Nan and Dillon?" Mom asked. "Did they have a nice time?"

"It was fine," I repeated, my voice clipped. Why did they always have to interrogate me about everything?

"Well." Mom clucked her tongue. "Excuse us for living."

"Sorry." To change the subject, I asked Dad, "When are you leaving for San Diego?"

Dad sold marketing software for an "up-and-coming" small business, as he liked to call it. I guess another business in San Diego was interested in using the software, and apparently this business was a big enough deal that the "up-and-coming" business felt it was worth it to send Dad there in person. Or something like that.

"Tomorrow."

"You going surfing while you're there?" I asked, trying to lighten the mood, which I'd actually ruined myself.

He chuckled. Dad was definitely not the surfing type. "Not sure I'll have time for surfing. Parasailing, though—now that's something I'd like to try."

Mom snorted. "Yeah right."

"Well, do you think you'll go to the beach?" I asked. I hadn't been to a beach since I was eight.

174

We'd gone to L.A. and taken the ferry to Catalina Island.

"Not sure."

"Well, if you do go to the beach, I have a solicitation for you. S-O-L-I-C-I-T-A-T-I-O-N."

Dad smiled. "Solicitate away, my dear."

"Solicit," I corrected. "I would like you to find me a piece of sea glass."

Dad tilted his head. "Sea glass, huh?"

"I can't remember what it looks like." There had been a souvenir shop on Catalina Island that sold all kinds of things made out of shells and sea glass, but we hadn't bought any of it.

"You could always google it," said Mom.

"I can't remember how it feels either. You can't feel it through Google."

"I shall do my best," Dad declared. Then he turned his attention to Mom. "Any special solicitations from you, my wife?"

"You just bring home that account. And the commission that goes with it. I want a new couch."

Dad saluted her. "I shall do my best."

chapter 21

Mormyridae.
M-O-R-M-Y-R-I-D-A-E.
Mormyridae.

"I learned something incredible this week," Dillon said to me. "It's going to blow your mind." It was only us two sitting in the media center eating lunch while Nan retook a math test with her teacher. She was already in algebra with the advanced eighth graders, and her teacher let them take tests twice if they wanted to, averaging the score.

"Is Vans having a big sale?" I asked.

Dillon rolled his eyes. "No, I wish. This is something that will blow *your* mind."

Nan plopped down at the table. "Hello, marvelous

persons." She swung her purple backpack onto the table and pulled out her lunch bag. "What are we talking about?"

"Done already, huh?" Dillon asked.

Nan snapped her fingers. "Easy as cake."

"Why is cake easy?" I asked. "They seem hard to bake." Not that I would know—I never ate cake.

"I dunno." Then she snapped her fingers again. "Easy as store-bought cake." She pulled out her yogurt and peeled the lid off, hitting Dillon's MTV T-shirt with little pink splatters.

He wiped his shirt with his hand. "Really, Nan?"

"Sorry." She shoved a plastic spoonful of pink into her mouth. "These things always explode when I open them."

"Maybe open them in private, then." He turned to me, still dramatically wiping his shirt even though no splatters were left on it. "Anyway, Avalyn, as I was saying—I thought you'd be interested in one of Pavel Belsky's videos this week."

"What was it about?" I asked.

"Mormyridae."

Nan and I looked at each other. "Mormon what?" she asked.

"Not Mormon." Dillon huffed. "Mormyridae."

I repeated the word. "Mormyridae. Mormyridae. How do you spell it?"

"M-O-R-M-Y-R-I-D-A-E."

"Good spelling word," I said.

"That's not why I thought you'd be interested."

"Well, what is it?"

"They're fish that produce electricity," he explained. "Also called elephant fish."

"Like electric eels." Nan threw her empty yogurt cup into her lunch bag and took out a bag of strawberries. She opened the bag and offered it to me. It always made me feel good when we could share food. I grabbed a strawberry and popped it into my mouth.

Dillon shook his head. "No. These fish are different. Eels use electricity to stun their prey."

"Like as a weapon." Nan did a karate chop in the air, a strawberry flying out of her fingers and hitting Dillon in the chest.

He held a hand to his chest as though injured. "Really?"

But Nan and I giggled. "Sorry," she said.

Dillon rubbed his chest. "I need a rain poncho when you eat around me. Anyway, I guess you can think of it as a weapon. Eels also use it to defend themselves."

Nan put her arm up in front of her face like a shield. "Defensive weapon." She was in a great mood. She must have aced that math test.

"I'm never going to be able to explain this if you insist on acting out everything I say," he complained.

Nan pursed her lips and ran a finger across them like a zipper.

"How do the elephant fish use electricity?" I asked.

"This is what I thought would interest you. They use it to communicate."

"Like telepathy," I said, getting excited. I knew it. I knew it was possible.

"If telepathy were real, electricity would be the only way it could happen."

I grabbed another strawberry out of Nan's plastic bag. "So how does it work?"

"The fish basically generate electrical pulses."

I popped the strawberry in my mouth and chewed on it, thinking over this information. "How do they know what the pulses mean?"

"This is what's so interesting. Scientists think their *pauses* are the most important part."

"Pauses?"

"Yeah, when they go quiet for a certain amount of time. It tells the listener they're about to communicate something important. It gets the listener's full attention so the ultimate message comes through clearly. They're pretty much always producing electricity, so it's the *pauses* in their electrical signals that communicate the most information."

"Like Mr. Griffin." Nan wrinkled her nose. "Like when everyone's acting all wild and he just stands up there quietly until we all stop talking and then he tells us something really important, like that he has a headache." She rolled her eyes.

"Actually," said Dillon. "Just like that."

I tapped my foot on the floor and drummed my fingers on the tabletop. "So, how do the other fish understand? I mean, how do they . . . *feel* the message?"

"They have receptors all over their bodies. Electroreceptors. And something else that's really interesting about them is that when scientists put one in a fish tank alone, it produced way fewer pauses. Like it was mumbling to itself all the time."

"Also like Mr. Griffin," said Nan. "I think I'm going to start calling him Mr. Elephant Fish."

Dillon stared her down until she made the zipper motion again.

"Now you're doing it," I said to Dillon. "Pausing like the elephant fish." I hadn't intended it as a joke, but Nan burst out laughing.

"Oh my gosh!" Dillon said loudly enough to echo through the media center, his face turning red with frustration. "You've been obsessed with telepathy for weeks, and now I'm trying to tell you important scientific information and you're not taking it seriously."

"Yes, I am." Anything, *anything*, that could give me some clue as to whether or not what I suspected with Adam was even remotely possible and that I wasn't making it all up in my head was important. "Please tell us the rest."

He sucked in a big breath. "What was I even saying?"

"The elephant fish mumbled like Mr. Griffin when it was alone in a tank," said Nan.

"Right. But when they put two together, one would always go silent when the other was talking."

"So they're polite fish." Nan smiled, cracker bits all over her teeth. Then she threw her hands in the air, a cracker in each one, and I half expected them to go flying and hit Dillon in the head. "Okay, okay. Would you rather?" Her eyes gradually narrowed and darted back and forth between me and Dillon. "Would you rather produce electricity that could be used as a weapon, or would you rather produce electricity to secretly communicate with people?"

Dillon and I grinned at each other. "Weapon," we said at the same time.

chapter 22

Incontrovertible.
I-N-C-O-N-T-R-O-V-E-R-T-I-B-L-E.
Incontrovertible.

I spotted Adam rushing out of school after my last class of the day, so I quickly waved goodbye to Nan and Dillon and hurried after him. I noticed how so many kids, too many kids, scratched their heads and grimaced and glared at him as he walked by. Even when the Meanie Butts weren't in sight, the damage they caused was all over the place. I wanted to scream at everyone to stop, and I wished I did have electrical powers I could zap them with whenever they acted mean. Like a shock collar for a dog.

Adam luckily didn't seem to notice what they

were doing. He continued walking, his head down, his arms crossed tightly over his chest. I reached him where the sidewalk turned to dirt. "Hey."

He looked up at me and slowed his pace. "Hey."

"How are you?"

He didn't say anything—just sort of shrugged a little bit.

I smiled. "I wonder if Bryden can still taste the dirt from the dance." I forced my voice to sound lighthearted, but I couldn't force away that sense of impending doom.

"I hope so," he said softly.

We walked quietly for a little bit before I finally asked, "Have you ever heard of Mormyridae?"

Adam shook his head. "What is it?"

"They're a kind of fish that can communicate with electricity. Sort of like Surge in X-Men. Dillon just told me all about them. He loves weird science stuff."

"Do the fish absorb the electricity?" Adam asked.

"No, I think they make it themselves."

"Then they're not really like Surge. She absorbs electricity."

"You mean like how Rogue can absorb powers?"

He nodded. "Surge has to get rid of the electricity, though, or it will build up too much in her body and she can lose control of it."

"Do you think…" How could I phrase this? My heart pounded, and I tried to keep my voice as casual as possible. "Do you think since fish can communicate by using electricity that it could ever be possible for people to do the same somehow? Or to even… like… *move* things with it?"

"You mean move things with electricity?"

"Sort of. Or maybe with their minds."

Adam furrowed his dark eyebrows and stopped, turning to me. "Why are you asking me this?"

I stopped, and we stared at each other for the longest time, my heart still thumping. I almost felt just then that we had some kind of understanding. That he knew I was like him. And I knew he was like me. But for some reason, we could never say it out loud.

I took a deep breath. "I'm asking because I do believe it."

Adam swallowed several times. "Why do you believe it?"

"Because…" I reached out a finger and gently touched his arm.

He flinched and gave me a strange look, pulling away and grabbing his arm as though I'd hurt him. But it was too late. I'd already felt everything, and I knew that whatever was down there in that dungeon, it was only getting worse.

He took slow, backward steps away from me, his face full of questions and confusion.

I breathed in, my heart feeling like it could burst through my chest, until I finally found the nerve to tell him, "I know something's wrong."

He backed farther away, his face darkening, his pale eyes shimmering. "You don't know anything about me," he said, his voice shaking. Then he ran away, leaving a trail of dust behind that grew and blew until the air was filled with it.

I ate a gluten-free, dairy-free potpie that night while sitting at my computer and waiting for Mom to bring Dad home from the airport. He'd called earlier in the day to let her know he'd gotten that account, and she'd clapped and twirled in the kitchen, so I knew whatever commission he would make off it was a big deal.

While I ate, I watched Pavel Belsky's video about Mormyridae. One fact Dillon had left out about the elephant fish was that they needed a lot of oxygen to feed their large brains, so if the water in Africa they lived in became less oxygenated, they could go extinct. Pavel said that could be a real possibility because of global warming. It was starting to feel like the elephant fish and I had a little too much in common. Made me wonder if the fate of the elephant fish was set in stone. Totally decided. Incontrovertible. I-N-C-O-N-T-R-O-V-E-R-T-I-B-L-E. Incontrovertible.

Or could it somehow be changed?

Mom and Dad got home when I had about a minute left of Pavel Belsky, so I paused the video. Dad nearly skipped into the living room. He put his suitcase down and gave me a big hug. The sparklers lit inside me, and it made me happy to know how happy he was.

When he pulled away, he said, "I found something for you."

"Oh." I squeezed my hands together. "My sea glass?"

"Yep." He walked back to his suitcase and opened it up. "Well, sort of." He rummaged through his clothes. "I couldn't find any on the beach, but I stopped in at a little souvenir shop and found this." He pulled out a bundle of tissue paper and handed it to me.

Inside the tissue paper was a small picture frame, the border made of a rainbow of sea glass. "Wow," I whispered, running my fingers around the frame, feeling the different pieces of sea glass that had been sanded cloudy and smooth. "I love it."

Mom stood next to me. "It's beautiful. What will you put in it?"

"I don't know yet." I continued running my fingers over the frame. "But I'll know when I find it."

chapter 23

Perturbation.
P-E-R-T-U-R-B-A-T-I-O-N.
Perturbation.

The air was awful the next morning. Mom was working another double shift, and Dad was sitting in front of his computer watching news videos. Dillon, Nan, and I were supposed to go watch Nan's older sister's soccer game together, but I had to cancel. Being outside for even a minute in this haze made my lungs tighten.

Last summer, we had a really bad desert fire that burned about a thousand acres right by us. The air was so thick with smoke that I couldn't even see the nearby hills and mountains. I'd had to stay indoors the whole time. The air looked like that today, but there was no fire.

I knew it was for the best that I didn't go to the game, but I couldn't stop thinking about Nan and Dillon being there without me. I imagined them cheering and high-fiving and buying hot dogs from the little food truck at the park. It all made me feel so completely hollow inside that I decided to ask Dad to play cards or Monopoly or something. As I walked through our living room, movement outside caught my eye.

Adam was in the road, rushing past our house. His shoulders were hunched, his arms folded tightly across his chest. He looked like he was in a real hurry. Where was he going, though? There was nowhere to go around here, especially in this awful weather. I opened my front door. "Adam!"

He didn't turn around, so I shouted his name louder. "Adam!"

He stopped, his shoulders still hunched. He wiped his face, then finally turned around. His eyes were red and swollen, like he'd been crying, but it could've been all the dust in the air.

"Where are you going?"

He looked from me, down the road, back to me. He shrugged his shoulders.

"Do you want to come in?" The wind suddenly gusted, spattering my eyes with dirt. I slammed them shut and rubbed them with my knuckles. "You should come in. It's horrible out here."

By the time I opened my irritated eyes, Adam was standing beside me. "Are you okay?" he asked softly.

I smiled. "Just got some dirt in my eyes. Come on." I motioned for him to follow me and shut the door against the wind.

Dad walked into the living room. "What's all the racket?"

I rubbed the corners of my eyes, trying to get the last of the dirt out. "This is Adam. Remember? I told you he just moved into the neighborhood."

"Right." Dad's face lit up. "Quiet Adam."

"Dad!"

"Oh, sorry." Dad looked sheepish. "I didn't know it was a secret."

But Adam forced a small smile and shook hands with Dad.

"Welcome to the neighborhood, Adam. You like it here?"

"It's okay." Adam's clipped tone didn't match his answer.

"So what brought you to our little Podunk town?" Dad asked, and I could sense Adam's discomfort with the question. He didn't look up, but his whole body tensed.

"I'm going to show Adam some of my comics," I said to take the pressure off him.

Dad must've seen that he was making Adam uncomfortable, too, because he didn't push the conversation. "Okay, then. Have fun. Nice meeting you, Adam."

Adam kept his eyes down. "Nice meeting you, too." His voice was so soft that I could barely even make out what he said.

As we walked away together, Dad called, "Keep the door open, please."

My face heated, and I rolled my eyes as we entered my room, being careful to push the door all the way open against the wall. "My dad is such a dork."

Adam wandered around my room, checking out the framed pictures that hung on my white walls. "He seems nice."

I snorted. "I guess." I thought of all the spelling

bee apps on Dad's phone and how most of them weren't free. Of doctor trips and special snacks for me and my friends and silly dance moves. "Yeah, he is."

"You're lucky."

"Hey, I'm sorry about yesterday. I—"

"Forget about it," Adam cut me off. Then he tapped one of the photos on my wall. "Who took this picture?"

I looked at the picture of Nan, Dillon, and me standing together, our arms wrapped around one another at Railroad Park in the city, where Dillon had celebrated his tenth birthday. "I don't remember. I think it was Dillon's mom."

"She has a good camera." His words were all so hushed.

"I guess you'd know. Do you have your camera with you?"

"Why?"

"You seem to have it with you a lot."

He turned back to the picture. "I'd never want to remember anything from today."

His answer stunned me. And also made me feel kind of bad. It was his first time visiting my house

after all, and I knew I would remember it. "Well…
did you want to see my comic book collection?"

He nodded, and we spent the next couple of hours
sitting on my bed, quietly reading my X-Men comics.
I noticed how careful he was not to get too near me.
He seemed to be afraid of accidentally bumping or
brushing me.

When we ran out of comics to read, I said, "Hey,
let's stream the first X-Men movie. I still haven't
watched it."

We sat down in the living room, and before we
were even halfway through the movie, I knew I
already liked it better than the newer ones because
Rogue was an important character. Rogue may have
started as a villain in the comic books, but she definitely wasn't a villain in this movie. She was just a
lonely, scared girl, afraid of anyone touching her. I
periodically glanced at Adam while we watched, but
he kept his face stoic the whole time.

The plot of the movie was basically that Magneto
wanted to use this weird machine to turn a bunch
of important political people into mutants because
there was a lot of discrimination happening against

the mutants. Magneto was worried about this because he was Jewish and had lived through the Holocaust. He understood how bad things could get when people discriminated against a certain group. Magneto was the villain, but he certainly didn't see himself as the villain. I honestly felt bad for Magneto and could see why he was doing what he was doing. He didn't feel all that villainous to me either. Did any villains realize they were villains?

Villainous is a really good spelling word. V-I-L-L-A-I-N-O-U-S. Villainous.

I guess where Magneto turned pretty bad was when he wanted to use Rogue to run the machine, knowing it would kill her. He allowed her to touch him so she could absorb his powers, and then he put her on the machine. I was pretty riveted by the end. Rogue did absorb Magneto's powers. And it cost her a lot. She ended up with that cool white streak in her hair, though. I kind of wished I had a white streak like that. My hair was so plain.

We sat in the living room quietly together watching it while Dad made burgers. "Are you staying with us for dinner, Adam?" Dad called from the kitchen.

Adam stared out the window, at the setting sun, as if the moment the sun was gone, monsters would appear in the darkness.

"Please stay," I said. "We have really good buns." I crinkled my nose. "Except they fall apart when you touch them."

Adam moved his eyes away from the window. "Why do they do that?"

"Gluten-free bread is like that, and I can't have gluten."

Dad stepped into the living room, a blob of ground beef in his hands. "But she can have delicious ground beef on sale. With all the fixings."

"But not mayo or cheese."

Dad patted and smooshed the beef between his hands. "But ketchup and mustard. And tomatoes and lettuce."

I looked at Adam with a hopeful smile, and he nodded.

"Great!" Dad announced, and I noticed he was wearing his *Mr. Good-Lookin' Is Cookin'* apron Mom had bought him for Christmas. My cheeks flushed in embarrassment. I hoped Adam didn't read it.

Adam was quiet while we ate, his pale eyes

constantly darting to the window and the fading light outside. It wasn't just fading because of the setting sun. The dust was getting heavier by the minute.

Dad, who had thankfully taken off his ridiculous apron, tried to start up a few conversations with Adam, but it was no use. When we finished eating, Dad offered to drive him home, but Adam refused, insisting it wasn't far, which I knew was true.

I walked Adam to the front door. "I'm really glad you came over," I said, feeling Dad spying from the kitchen. "It was fun, right?"

Adam stood in front of the door, shifting from foot to foot, his eyes downcast. "Yes."

"Maybe you could come back again?"

He kept his eyes down and nodded. Then I opened the door to let him out, closing it softly behind him. From the living room window, I watched him walk across the lighted yard before disappearing into the darkness.

Dad came up beside me, patting my back. "He seems like a nice boy. You were right—very quiet. Who did he say he lives with?"

I studied the darkness, even though I couldn't see Adam anymore. "He didn't." I'd wanted to ask him again, but he seemed to get so upset when I'd brought it up before. All I knew for certain was that whoever it was, whoever or whatever he was going home to, it filled him with dread. I didn't even need to touch him to know that.

"Perturbation," I whispered to the darkness. "P E R T U R B A T I O N. Perturbation."

chapter 24

Epiphany.
E-P-I-P-H-A-N-Y.
Epiphany.

The dust woke me in the middle of the night. I'd been having the dream again—the one of the room made of cloudy glass walls, the room that continued to grow smaller and more suffocating. I startled awake, gasping for air, the dust outside blowing so hard that I thought for sure it would break through my window. I got up, coughed, caught my breath, then turned the air filter up as high as it would go, but it didn't have a setting high enough for what was happening—an "apocalyptic dust storm" setting.

I'd used my peak flow meter before bed, and the

numbers were the worst since I'd started using it again—all yellow, but not yet in red. I'd never gone into red before, but I was closer to reaching it than ever.

Picking up the sea glass frame from my bedside table, I ran my fingers over the glass, feeling its smoothness, wondering what each piece had been—a beer bottle? A jelly jar? A window? I wondered how long it had taken for the glass to change from sharp and piercing to soft and smooth.

I put down the frame and went to the window, pressed my hands to it, as though I could stop the dust from breaking through. Day after day the glass had become more and more cloudy, no matter how many times Mom washed it and wiped it down with glass cleaner, a frustrated scowl on her face as she scrubbed and rubbed and streaked paper towel across it.

Mom's efforts to clean the glass were pointless. The blowing sand had been etching it, marking it, and gradually wearing it away, just as I'd feared the night I asked Dillon if it were possible. It was happening just like my dream.

But it wasn't taking a long time as Dillon had

thought. It wasn't taking years. Dillon didn't know everything about the world. Dillon didn't know a lot about what was impossible. And what was possible.

Tonight, I could see letters reflected in the glass: *E, P, I, P, H, A, N, Y.*

My quivering hands pressed against the shuddering glass—the thinning, sandblasted glass—its clarity dimming, my heart drumming and lungs whistling. For the first time, I didn't ask, *What is happening?*

The question on my mind and heart and lips that night was, *What is happening to you?*

chapter 25

Panacea.
P-A-N-A-C-E-A.
Panacea.

I took off school the following Monday so Dad could take me back to the allergist. We sat side by side in the waiting room, a HEPA filter whirring in the corner. "That's like the Cadillac of HEPA filters," Dad whispered to me, even though we were the only people in the waiting room. "Mom's been talking about it for a while now. Maybe it's time we order one for your room."

"Sure."

Dad walked over to the filter and pulled out his phone, googling to see where he could buy one. His eyes grew large. He sat back down next to me and I saw his screen.

"That's a lot of money, Dad," I said.

But Dad ordered it anyway. "Can't place a price on your health, Avalyn." He put an arm around me and squeezed.

I buried my face in his shirt and hugged him back, uttering a muffled "Thank you."

He put a hand to his heart and let out a loud breath. "Thank goodness I got that commission."

A nurse came out and called my name, and we followed her back to a small room, where she took my temperature, weight, height, and blood pressure. Then Dad and I sat in the small room quietly. He read a magazine he'd grabbed from the waiting room, and I read the poster on the back of the door: THE 14 ALLERGENS.

I was allergic to half the foods on there. Funny—I didn't know mustard was a common allergen, and I'd have gladly traded any of my allergens for that one. Or crustaceans. Or mollusks, whatever that was. It looked like a clam. Why did I have to have all the worst allergies? At least if I were allergic to mustard and clams, I could still have pizza.

"Life is so unfair," I muttered.

Dad looked up from his magazine and followed my gaze to the poster. "At least you can have celery, honey." He waggled his eyebrows at me. "So...not so unfair after all, I'd say."

"Celery's gross," I grumped.

The doctor finally entered the room. "Hey there, Avalyn."

I swung my legs, the table paper crunching under me. "Hi, Dr. Abrams."

"Sounds like you're still having some trouble," he said, looking over whatever was on his clipboard.

I swung my legs harder. "Yeah...from the dust, I think."

He nodded. "I saw on the news it's been extra dusty up north where you live." He looked at Dad. "That's sort of unusual, isn't it?"

"Yes, it is," Dad said. "We've never had this much dust, especially this time of year."

"How often have you had to use your rescue inhaler?" Dr. Abrams asked.

I looked at Dad, and he nodded. "Every day," I said.

The doctor raised an eyebrow. "More than once?"

"I'd say…three or four times."

That didn't seem to make him very happy. "That's a lot, Avalyn. And the nebulizer?"

"Almost every night," Dad said. "That's when the dust seems to blow the hardest."

He stuck the nose light thingy up my nostril. "You've been having a lot more congestion?"

"It's the worst at night."

He nodded. "That's pretty common. Open wide." Then he looked down my throat, the tongue depressor making me gag a little. "A good allergy nose spray could help with all this sinus drainage I'm seeing back there."

Then Dr. Abrams had me blow into the peak flow meter, which was way fancier than mine at home, and even though I blew my hardest, it was still in yellow. I hadn't been able to get it into green at home for days now. He had me try a few more times, his frown deepening with each new reading. "Have you been keeping a log as I asked?"

I took out my phone and pulled up my breathing log. You could literally see how the dust had been increasing over time, my readings falling every day. Dr. Abrams sat down in a chair and scrolled through my breathing log, scratching his cheek. "This doesn't look great."

Dr. Abrams entered my numbers into the computer while Dad and I sat there quietly, periodically glancing at each other. Then he whirled to face us in the swivel chair. "I think we should discuss the oral medication again."

Dad adamantly shook his head. "Last resort," he said. We'd looked up the medication Dr. Abrams wanted me to try, and the side effects were scary: anxiety, memory loss, depression, and even suicidal tendencies? What was the point of taking medication to save your life if that medication might make you want to end your life? "The side effects are terrifying."

"I think the number of times she's using her rescue inhaler right now is terrifying," Dr. Abrams said. "Avalyn, your airways are badly inflamed right now, and your lung function is worse than it's been in a long time. I think it's time to start looking at those 'last resort' options."

"No panacea," I mumbled. "P-A-N-A-C-E-A. Panacea."

Dr. Abrams smiled down at me, and Dad said, "Avalyn's preparing for a spelling bee."

"Ah, I see."

"I'll just avoid my triggers," I said.

"What triggers *haven't* you been avoiding?" Dr. Abrams asked.

The truth was, the one big trigger was unavoidable, and everyone knew it.

"I won't go outside anymore." I knew as soon as I said it, this was impossible. How would I get from class to class? In one of those bubble things? That would be even more embarrassing than wearing the WordGirl bandana.

Dr. Abrams sighed. "That's no way to live, Avalyn. You need time outside to be healthy. And besides, you know as well as I do that the dust gets into everything. You can't avoid it as long as this weather persists. Tell you what—pick up some N95 masks and let's try the nasal spray. Start doing the nebulizer every night before bed and every morning when you get up for the next two weeks. Absolutely avoid all trigger foods—"

"I always do."

"Good." He looked at his clipboard. "That's really good, but I see you haven't had a food allergy test in a couple of years. I think we should do a new one. There could be some things we're missing."

"Sounds good," said Dad.

I groaned. Was I the only one who didn't think it sounded good? The last thing I needed was to find out there were more foods I couldn't eat.

"Then you come back in two weeks, and we'll reassess everything."

"Maybe by then the air will have cleared up, too," said Dad hopefully.

But no matter how many times we all said it, I didn't think the air was going to clear up. Nothing could make the air clear up until I figured out what was causing it—and how to stop it.

chapter 26

Evanescent.
E-V-A-N-E-S-C-E-N-T.
Evanescent.

The air was so bad all the time now that I wasn't walking to and from school anymore; Mom or Dad always drove me. That meant I no longer got a chance to see Adam outside of school, and he was getting harder to track down. I wondered whether he was deliberately avoiding me.

I finally found him in the media center at lunchtime one day. He wasn't eating, though. He had a stack of X-Men comics in front of him.

I set my backpack down on the floor and sat across from him. "Hey."

Nan and Dillon had decided to brave the cafeteria for pizza day, so we were almost completely alone. It was quiet other than the sounds of Ms. Lund rummaging around at her desk and typing on her computer from time to time.

He didn't look up, but he did mumble back, "Hey."

"Where've you been?"

He shrugged. "Around."

"But you haven't been in social studies. If I knew your phone number, I would've called to see where you were, and—"

"I've been sick."

"Oh...what did you have?"

"Nothing serious."

"Oh," I said again. "That's good. I'm glad you're better." I drummed my fingers on the table. "I've been wanting to ask you if you want to come over and watch the next X-Men movie with me."

He shrugged again.

"I ordered it. Just been...waiting to see if you want to watch it with me. Like...together."

He turned the page of his comic book, his eyebrows drawn together. I looked down and saw that he was reading another comic with Sooraya Qadir. I

210

tapped the picture of her. "I thought you liked Wind Dancer better."

He finally spoke, his voice quiet. "They don't have any comics with Wind Dancer."

"Maybe we should get some." I pulled out my phone and searched until I found a website that sold old comics. "Sofia Mantega," I mumbled to myself. "This one's only three dollars. Should I get it?" I held the phone up for him.

He barely glanced up, then looked back down at his comic. "If you want to."

I'd have to ask Mom or Dad to use their credit card. "K. I'll order it when I get home." Then I began scrolling through the pictures until I stopped on one with Wind Dancer floating, or maybe flying. Wind, or maybe it was dust, whirled around her. I held the phone closer to my face to study the picture. It reminded me of the day we'd gotten caught in the sudden dust devil. The day Bryden had stolen my inhaler. The day that Adam—

"What is it?"

I put the phone down. Adam was staring at me, his eyes intense. I showed him the picture. "She looks powerful."

"She is." His low voice shook. His lips trembled a little. His eyes turned glassy.

Adam's happiness the night of the dance, and sometimes when we talked on our way to and from school, and every other time I thought I may have glimpsed it, had been a spark that kept getting put out as quickly as it lit. It didn't even last as long as a real sparkler. It was evanescent. E-V-A-N-E-S-C-E-N-T. Evanescent.

Someone was snuffing it out. And I wasn't sure anymore it was the Meanie Butt Band. What was happening during the worst dust storms? Who was with him at night when the dust blew so hard?

We looked at each other a long time before I finally asked him, "Are you okay?"

He swallowed. Nodded. Looked back down at his comic and turned the page.

"Do you miss your mom?"

He looked up, his mouth hung open, as though he couldn't believe I'd ask such a stupid question. "Of course I do."

I did feel kind of stupid now. "Do you have a picture of her I could see?"

"No."

His answer startled me. "You don't want to show me a picture?"

His voice rose. "No, I don't have any pictures."

Ms. Lund walked past us, toward the big windows. "It's really picking up out there," she said.

I glanced at the windows and saw that the palo verde branches had started whipping around wildly. I turned back to Adam. "But...didn't you take any of her with your camera?"

"No."

"But...why?"

"Why do you always have to ask so many questions?" His eyes were growing glassy again, his face reddening.

I hated that I seemed to upset him with my questions, but how could I figure all this out if I didn't ask any? "I'm sorry," I whispered, crossing my arms over my chest, biting the inside of my lip. "I wish you would ask me some sometimes."

His face softened a little. "She was always sad, okay? She was never, ever *not* sad. And I only take pictures of things I want to remember. Okay?"

I nodded. "Okay. Why do you think she was so sad all—"

"Stop asking questions!" His voice echoed through the quiet media center. Ms. Lund whirled around from the window, her face full of surprise and concern. But before she could say anything, Adam grabbed his bag and ran off.

The wind outside whirled and whipped and darkened. I looked down at the comic book on the table, at the picture of Sooraya Qadir, and then back out the window.

"What was that all about?" asked Ms. Lund.

I swallowed and blinked back the hot tears forming. "I don't know."

"He seems really upset."

I nodded but kept my gaze on the window. "I don't think he feels well."

"Oh yeah?"

"Yeah.... He said he's been sick."

Ms. Lund moved back around the counter. "Maybe he should go see Ms. Imani, then." She picked up the phone and asked the person on the line to page Adam to go to the nurse's office. Then she put the phone down. "Maybe his uncle can come pick him up."

I jolted and looked away from the window. "Uncle? He lives with his uncle?"

"Uh-huh," she said absentmindedly, pushing a stack of books from one side of her desk to the other. Then she looked up at me. "I thought you two were friends. Didn't you know?"

I shook my head. "I really don't know him at all."

Later, in social studies, I tried to catch his eye as he walked in, but Adam ignored me. He skulked to his desk in the back and put his head down on his arms as he always did. I guessed he must've told Ms. Imani he wasn't sick after all.

When class was finally over, Adam jumped up and rushed out. I packed up my stuff as quickly as I could and swung my backpack over my shoulder, hurrying after him. I wanted to apologize for prying so much, but maybe that was just more prying. Maybe letting him cool off was the best thing.

I was about twenty feet behind him when suddenly someone hocked up a loogie and spit it on Adam's cheek.

Adam kept walking. He didn't even wipe the spit from his face.

I wanted to scream at him from where I stood

frozen. I wanted to scream at Adam, but not at the nameless kid. I wanted to scream at Adam to shout, yell, fight back, stand up for himself.

How can you do nothing?

How can you say nothing?

How can you act like you're nothing?

And then I remembered Valerie licking her hand and wiping it on my neck as she walked by me in language arts.

Remembered Bryden picking up my lunch bag and spitting into it, ruining my food.

Remembered Caleb using the corner of my T-shirt to blow his nose.

And I remembered me sitting there.

Doing nothing.

Saying nothing.

Being nothing.

Just like Adam, who kept walking, the layer of dust on the sidewalk lifting and swirling around him.

chapter 27

Despondency.
D-E-S-P-O-N-D-E-N-C-Y.
Despondency.

I caught up to Nan and Dillon as soon as I reached school the next morning. "Hello, marvelous persons," I said, though my tone probably didn't match the words. That building feeling of dread was not going away. It was only getting worse. I always felt like the day we saw the first dust storm. Like something bad was coming. Something really bad.

"Hello, marvelous person," Dillon said. Then he reached out and touched my cheek. "You don't look so good. You have big dark rings under your eyes."

I turned away from his hand. "I'm totally fine, *Dad*."

Nan scrunched her eyebrows. "Maybe you should go home, Avalyn."

"I said I'm fine." I wanted to change the subject. "Guess what? It's my parents' anniversary tomorrow night, which means they're going out for dinner, which also means we can have the whole house to ourselves. They'll probably stay out late, too." I bounced from foot to foot. "*Marble Mountain Rescue* marathon," I squealed.

Marble Mountain Rescue was our favorite show, and I couldn't think of a better way to escape everything right now than getting totally lost in the drama. It was about a group of teenagers who worked as rescuers in the Marble Mountains of California. That wasn't the exciting part, though. The exciting part was finding out whether Alicia and Jackson were going to finally get together, especially after they'd rescued this girl named Celeste who was pretending to be someone she wasn't and clearly had a thing for Jackson. It was kind of complicated, but the new season had just gotten released, and I couldn't wait to figure out all the plot twists. It would only take us fourteen hours to binge it. I'd calculated it.

Dillon and Nan were quiet as they gave each other a look like they had a secret between them—a secret that didn't include me.

I stopped my excited bouncing. "What?"

"It's nothing, Avalyn," said Nan. "It's just that...I already have plans for tomorrow night."

I turned my head to Dillon. "What about you?"

He twisted his face, looked up at the sky, then down at his Tom and Jerry Vans. "I have plans, too."

"Separate plans?" I stook a step back. "Or plans together?"

"It's no big deal," Nan said. "My uncle got us free tickets to the monster truck show coming to Phoenix."

I took another step back. "And I'm not invited?"

"It's not like that," Dillon said quickly. "We talked about it, and there'll be a ton of fumes and dust and stuff in the air. We thought it would be best to not even tell you so you wouldn't feel left out like you always do."

"And you've had so much breathing trouble lately," added Nan. "We wouldn't want you to get sicker or anything and have to miss more school than you already have."

My face heated and my vision blurred. "Well, that was really good thinking. Because I definitely don't feel left out now." I pushed between the two of them and stormed away, not even sure where I was heading.

"Avalyn!" I heard them both call, but I didn't look back.

Like it wasn't bad enough that my parents were always hovering and deciding what I should and shouldn't do because of my asthma. Now my best friends were doing it, too.

Later that day, I made my way to the media center so I could help Ms. Lund with yearbook stuff, which I'd badly neglected lately. I spotted Adam sitting at a desk. Sometimes it seemed that he was the only person who felt more alone than I did. And even though I didn't want Adam to be or feel so alone, it also somehow made me feel better to be around him feeling alone. I just hoped he wasn't still mad at me. I knew not to ask about his uncle.

I walked over and put my backpack down. "What are you working on?"

He pushed the stack of pictures my way without saying anything.

"Adam took some nice pictures of the dance." Ms. Lund smiled in a satisfied way. "I gave him the assignment, and he really came through."

I flipped through the pictures—there were shots of the decorations and the snack table and of Dr. Delgado and Ms. Lund dancing together. They looked like they were laughing. There were also shots of some kids dancing, but none of the Meanie Butt Band, and I remembered what he'd said to me—about how he only ever took pictures of the things he wanted to remember.

As I sifted through the stack of pictures again, searching, letters filled my insides: *D, E, S, P, O, N, D, E, N, C, Y.*

There were also no pictures of me.

chapter 28

Metamorphosis.
M-E-T-A-M-O-R-P-H-O-S-I-S.
Metamorphosis.

The weekend stunk big time. I couldn't stop thinking about Nan and Dillon going to the monster truck show without me. About Adam and the pictures he'd taken. And not taken. I'd thought he was starting to like me. I'd thought, maybe, we were becoming friends. That I was *this* close to figuring everything out.

Now it felt like I was back at the beginning with nothing but unanswered questions as the dust got worse and worse.

I watched the rest of the old X-Men movies. They were okay but not nearly as good as the first one, since

Rogue wasn't in them as much. I also read the X-Men comic when Rogue kisses her boyfriend for the first time and nearly kills him. That made me remember what Adam had said about wishing some people would die when they touched him. More unanswered questions.

I watched some Pavel Belsky videos on YouTube, but those only made me think of Dillon. I wished Pavel Belsky could explain to me what was happening with Adam and the dust, but he hadn't made any videos on telepathy or telekinesis. I could practically hear Dillon in his know-it-all voice: *That's not real science, Avalyn, and Pavel Belsky only investigates real scientific topics.* It was funny how you could miss someone and be annoyed by them at the same time.

When I got sick of all things X-Men and Pavel Belsky, I lay on my bed and stared out my foggy window at the big saguaro outside. It hadn't bloomed last spring, and I wondered if this year would be the same. It was starting to look a little yellow. Mom said it could be dying from the drought.

The recent wildfires had killed thousands of saguaros, and the ones that were left were starting to die from drought. It took hundreds of years for a saguaro to grow as big as the one outside my window. If they all died off, would they ever be able to come back?

The desert was changing. Transforming. Transfiguring.

"Metamorphosis," I whispered to myself, still staring at the cactus outside my window. "M-E-T-A-M-O-R-P-H-O-S-I-S. Metamorphosis."

Nothing made sense anymore.

chapter 29

Impuissant.
I-M-P-U-I-S-S-A-N-T.
Impuissant.

"Hey," Dillon called, catching up to me outside after class on Monday.

I stopped and turned, trying to keep my face unreadable. The air was hazy, and my lungs felt tight. I needed to get to my next class. I pulled out my inhaler and took a puff.

He made a smile that twitched at the corners of his mouth. "Hello, marvelous person. You okay?"

"I'm fine. I don't need anyone worrying about me. So did you guys have fun at the monster truck show?"

Dillon flinched, which was what I'd hoped for. "No, not really. It was super loud, and some drunk guy splattered us with beer, and Nan dropped her hot dog, and we felt bad all night. We should've asked you to come, even if you couldn't. We still should've asked." He stuck his lip out and made puppy dog eyes at me. "Forgive us, please."

I bit my smile away. "The puppy dog face isn't working, I'll have you know"

He jutted his lip out even more.

I shook my head, still trying not to smile. "Nope. Still not working."

He dropped the look, his face serious now. "You had every right to be upset."

"It's just…I know it stinks sometimes being friends with me."

He shook his head enthusiastically. "It never stinks being friends with you."

"I get it," I said. "I can't hang out in your houses or eat a pizza with you or anything."

Dillon kicked my plain white tennis shoe with his colorful one. It had the periodic table in several colors all over it. A little burst of warmth went up my leg. "But we can come to your house and share a fake pizza with you."

"If you're okay with that," I said.

Dillon drew his eyebrows together. "Why wouldn't I be?"

Right then, Bryden and Caleb walked up behind Dillon. Bryden stopped and pretended to cough, sneaking the word "girl" into it.

Dillon's face instantly fell. "That's fine," he said without turning around. "Some of my favorite people are girls." He forced a smile at me, but I couldn't muster one myself, not with Bryden and Caleb standing right behind Dillon, making me feel even more suffocated than I already did.

"Really?" Bryden said. "That's good news. Because we have a present for you, *girl*."

Bryden reached into his backpack and pulled something out—a large white bra. "Come here, girl."

Dillon finally turned around. "Am I supposed to be scared of a bra?" He stood up straighter, gripping the straps of his backpack so tightly his knuckles were white.

Then Bryden grabbed Dillon by the arm while

Caleb yanked Dillon's backpack off. I looked around frantically, hoping for a teacher or someone to come outside, but kids were gathering around now, blocking the three boys from view.

Once Caleb got Dillon's backpack off, Bryden twisted Dillon's arm, and Dillon cried out in pain. Then they forced one of the bra straps over Dillon's shoulder. And then the other.

What could I do? What could I do? "Stop it," I croaked, but the words caught in my dry throat, in my tight lungs, barely audible to anyone but me.

The boys were having a hard time with the bra clasp, so while Caleb held Dillon's arms, Bryden tied the back into a tight knot. Once they were sure the knot would hold, they finally released him, pushing him away and making him stumble to the ground.

Dillon stood back up wearing the bra in front of the whole circle of kids who had gathered to see what was happening.

Someone whistled.

Another person called out, "Hey, sexy lady!"

And then a bunch of kids started clapping while Dillon held himself upright, shoulders back, jutting out his chin, which quivered. When his eyes started

228

glistening, he grabbed his backpack and, swinging it over his shoulder, pushed his way through the crowd.

It took a second for my feet to move. I ran after him across campus, where I spotted him slamming his way into a boys' bathroom. I stood outside for a minute, debating whether to go in or not. I took a puff of my inhaler. When no one came out for a while, I eased the door open. It looked completely empty, so I slipped inside.

Dillon's soft sniffling echoed off the tiled floor and walls. I walked along the stalls, bending over to look for the colorful periodic table on his shoes. I didn't find it, but only one stall was closed and locked, and the white bra lay on the floor next to the toilet. The sniffles quieted when I gently knocked on the door.

"It's me," I whispered. The lock slowly turned, and I pushed the door open, locking it behind me.

Dillon sat on the toilet, his legs pulled up to his chest so his shoes rested on the seat. Tears ran down his cheeks. I bent down and put my arms around him. My body flooded with so much pain and sadness that I started crying too, which seemed to make Dillon stop.

"Why are *you* crying?" he asked in an almost accusatory tone.

"I'm just so sorry for what they did." For a brief moment, the pain and sadness coming from Dillon seemed to ease a little before it began overflowing again.

"Why do they hate us so much, Avalyn?" he sobbed into my shoulder.

I didn't answer him. I didn't think he expected an answer in the first place, since neither of us could answer that question. I mean, I could tell Dillon they hated him because of who he was and what he wore. I could tell him they hated me because of how I was born. They hated Adam because of how he looked when he arrived at school. They hated Nan because of where her family came from.

So I could tell Dillon the who, what, how, when, and where of their hating us. But what I could never, ever tell him was the why.

"I'm sorry," I said again, squeezing him tightly.

Dillon put his feet down and gently pushed me away, wiping his eyes and standing up from the toilet to face me, his cheeks bright red and damp. "It's fine. I don't care."

"Yes, you do. But you shouldn't."

"Why not?"

"Because you're better than all of them. You're a marvelous person, a genius who's going to change the whole world. Who are they? What are they ever going to do?"

Dillon stared at me, and I was surprised at the fury in his eyes. "Whatever they want, Avalyn." His words were like a stab of anger to my heart. "Because who's going to stop them?"

He stormed past me out of the stall, stomping toward the bathroom door. He started to push it open but stopped. "You just watched," he said, facing away from me, both his hands flat against the door, his voice trembling. "You just stood there and watched."

I wanted to tell him that it wasn't true. That it hadn't been a choice. That I'd wanted to tell them to stop. That the words had caught in my throat. That my feet had been glued to the sidewalk and that I'd been unable to move. That Bryden and Caleb weren't just way stronger than Dillon, they were way stronger than me, too. I was totally impuissant. I-M-P-U-I-S-S-A-N-T. Impuissant. So what could I have done anyway?

"You didn't say *anything*." Every word Dillon spoke was slow and drawn out and filled with anger and accusation. Then he pushed the door open forcefully, leaving me alone in the quiet boys' bathroom.

Dillon was wrong that I hadn't said anything while they bullied him. No. Not bullied. While they *assaulted* him in front of everyone.

Like the elephant fish, my silence said *everything*.

chapter 30

Paroxysm.
P-A-R-O-X-Y-S-M.
Paroxysm.

I stared at my dinner: grilled chicken, rice, and broccoli. I didn't have any kind of appetite, and the boring dinner wasn't helping. Clanging my fork against my plate over and over, I couldn't stop thinking about Dillon and what they'd done to him. And what I'd done. Which was nothing. Nothing at all.

"You okay, honey?" Mom asked.

I continued clanking my fork and staring at my plate.

That bra around Dillon's chest. I could feel how it had squeezed him. I felt all of it when I hugged him.

The pain. The embarrassment. The fear of leaving the stall. The anger.

And then there was me, just watching it all happen. Quiet. Silent. Noiseless. Soundless. Mute. Speechless. Voiceless.

Unspeaking. Unspeaking. Unspeaking.

"Avalyn?" Dad asked. "You all right?"

I dropped my fork and rolled my eyes. "Why do you have to be such helicopter parents?"

Dad dropped his own fork and pushed his plate of half-eaten chicken forward. "Excuse me? Did you really just say that?"

"Yes, I said exactly what you heard."

Both of them stared at me, as if an alien had suddenly burst right out of my chest like in this movie Dillon and Nan and I had secretly watched a few years ago. We'd all had nightmares about it for weeks afterward but couldn't tell our parents because then we'd get in trouble for having watched it in the first place.

I felt like Surge. Like electricity was building, building, building inside me and I was about to lose control of it if I didn't let it out. "Did it ever occur to you that I get really sick of you hovering over me every second?" I said. "You make me feel like I'm always on the verge of death."

"We just asked if everything was okay," Mom said, her voice rising. "That's all. We didn't ask if you needed to go the doctor or hospital or anything. You've been really quiet, and you look upset. That's all."

Yeah—I was very, very upset. I was upset about what had happened to Dillon, and the secret of it all burned, scorching my insides, on the verge of exploding out of my chest like the alien in that movie. I wanted to tell someone, anyone, about what had happened. But what would that accomplish? It was all so pointless.

"I don't care what's going on that's causing you to behave like this," said Dad. "You don't talk to us like that."

"Or what?" I pushed away from the table. "You'll ground me? From what? I can't go anywhere. I can't go to Nan's or Dillon's house. I can't go outside because the dust is so bad. What are you going to ground me from?"

Dad stood up to face me. "How about from Big Brother?"

I stomped over to the kitchen counter and picked up the phone and handed it to Dad. "Here you go. Not like I have anyone to talk to anyway."

Mom still sat at the table, looking totally bewildered. "Are you…stressed out about the spelling bee?"

"I don't care about the stupid spelling bee." That was a huge lie.

Dad gripped my phone in his hands. "Don't say that. We know how important it is to you."

My eyes darted back and forth between them. "The only reason I spell is because I can't do anything else."

"What are you talking about?" Mom's voice sounded small. "You can do all kinds of things."

"No, I can't!" I shouted. "I can't do sports. I can't ride horses like everyone else around here. I can't… go to a monster truck show!"

Dad's eyes were wide with hurt and confusion. "I didn't know you wanted to go to a monster truck show."

"I don't!" I wiped the tear from my cheek. "It's already over. It just would've been nice to have had the option, you know?"

Dad's lip turned up at one corner. "Tim up the

street has a truck with huge tires out in his yard. Maybe he can bring it over here and do wheelies in the driveway."

"Trucks don't do wheelies!" I stomped my foot like a little kid. "And I'm really sick and tired of your… of your… raillery!" Before Mom or Dad could react, I ran to my room and slammed the door.

I threw myself down on my bed and pulled my comforter up to my chin, slamming my head back against my padded headboard. I wished it had been wood so it could have made a loud banging noise and hurt at least a little bit.

The truth was, the person I was maddest at— absolutely furious at—was myself. Because I knew deep down inside that the real reason I didn't tell Mom and Dad or anyone else about what had happened to Dillon wasn't because it was pointless. It was because I would have to admit that I'd just stood there and watched it all happen.

I was still sitting in the same exact position, my head pressed against my padded headboard about an hour later when there was a soft knock on my door.

Dad walked in and sat on the bed, on top of my legs, which were buried under the covers. I squirmed my feet and grunted to let him know he was bothering me. He stood and walked to my dresser. He picked up the sea glass frame and tapped the glass. "You haven't put a picture in here yet."

I grunted again. I'd thought maybe I'd use a picture of me and Dillon and Nan, but I wasn't sure anymore.

"How about you put a picture of me in there?" He set the frame down and pulled my phone out of his pocket. He took a cheesy, smiling selfie and showed it to me. "Now that's one for the frame." He tapped a few more things on the phone. "And also for this." He handed the phone back to me so I could see that he'd changed my lock screen from the picture of my friends and me to the selfie he just took.

I rolled my eyes and threw the phone down on my comforter. Dad sat back on the bed, careful to avoid my legs. "That was a good word," he said. "*Raillery*, I mean. R-A-I-L-L-E-R-Y. Good-natured teasing, right?"

"What did you do?" I muttered. "Google it?"

"Yes, I did." Dad cleared his throat. "The

238

word that came to *my* mind was actually *paroxysm.*
P-A-R-O-X-Y-S-M."

I turned my head away. "I'm not in a spelling mood."

"Well, are you in a monster truck mood? Because I also googled that, and we can watch them do wheelies on YouTube. Not that I'm trying to prove I'm right or anything. I would never do that." He whistled all casually. "I would never try to prove myself right."

I could feel him smiling at me, and I turned my head like an owl farther away from him. "I don't actually care about monster trucks," I said to my headboard.

"Then what was that all about, Avalyn? You know you really hurt Mom's feelings."

I turned to him, mostly because my neck was starting to hurt. "Well, I am sorry about that, but Nan and Dillon went to the monster truck show together on Saturday and they didn't even invite me."

Dad's smile fell. "Why not? Did you guys have a fight?"

"No. They didn't invite me because of fumes and dust and stuff."

"Oh," Dad said softly. "So they were thinking of your health."

I nodded.

"But that doesn't make you feel any better, does it?"

"No. But I'm not mad about it anymore."

Dad raised an eyebrow. "You seem mad about it still."

I *was* mad. Mad at myself for being a coward. Mad at Mom and Dad for being so overprotective. And yes, I guess I was still mad at Nan and Dillon for not inviting me. For sharing cookies I couldn't eat. For going to each other's houses when they know I couldn't come. For living totally normal lives without me.

I stared at my sandblasted window. "I guess I'm just mad at the whole world." Everything outside my room looked fuzzy and foggy. I couldn't see anything clearly anymore.

"It's okay to feel that way sometimes," said Dad. "The world can be a real jerk."

"The world *is* a jerk. A big fat mean stinking jerk." Especially when it was filled with dust.

chapter 31

Vengeance.
V-E-N-G-E-A-N-C-E.
Vengeance.

I stared out the living room window the next morning, waiting for Adam to walk by before Mom drove me to school. I wasn't ready to give up on this. On him. On the dust. But he never showed. Then I couldn't find him at school. He'd been gone a lot, and the dust was getting worse all the time.

I couldn't bring myself to face Dillon after what had happened, and the truth was, I was still hurt about the whole monster truck thing. It made me wonder how many times they'd done stuff together without inviting me or telling me. It could have been *thousands* of times for all I knew. And I guess, the more I thought about the monster truck thing, the less I had to think about the bra thing.

I walked down the sidewalk at school, totally caught up in thinking about Dillon and Nan and Adam, when suddenly dirt started raining down on me. I stopped, frozen, holding my breath, as pebbles and dried weeds cascaded over my hair and face in a thick brown waterfall. I pressed my hands over my mouth to try to keep from sucking the dust into my lungs.

"Payback, Wheezer," Valerie hissed in my ear before she and Emma ran off laughing, the empty pink child's play bucket dangling in her hand.

I stared down at the pile of dirt at my feet. In my mind, it had formed into the letters *V, E, N, G, E, A, N, C, E.*

Several kids stopped. Some of them snickered. Some pointed and whispered. Others stared at me, their mouths hanging open in shock. Wordless. Voiceless. Soundless.

Unspeaking. Unspeaking. Unspeaking.

Just as always. It was the same scene day after day after day. Nothing ever changed.

chapter 32

Excruciation.
E-X-C-R-U-C-I-A-T-I-O-N.
Excruciation.

I hurried to the bathroom and tried to pick the dirt out of my hair, but the sand had gotten into everything— my ears, my shirt, my eyes, my mouth, my nose. The longer I stood there trying to pick it out, the more I could feel that electricity building inside me, about to explode. About to lose control. About to snap.

The school day wasn't over, but I put on my N95 mask and left without telling anyone. I just walked right off campus and went home.

The moment I stepped through the door, I darted for the shower and turned the water to blazing hot.

As I washed the dirt out of my hair, it was hard to tell how hard I was actually crying because of the water running down my face and into my eyes.

After I was done getting dressed, I sat in the living room and stared out the window at the haze, waiting for the inevitable texts from Mom and Dad.

Why are you home?

How did you get home?

Why aren't you at school?

Are you okay?

But my phone was quiet. The house was quiet. Outside was quiet. My breath was quiet. But my mind was roaring loud. It felt like a dust storm blowing inside me, making me wobble and shake. Like Surge, the electricity had built up inside me to the point of explosion.

I couldn't stand to sit in this house. I couldn't stand to wonder anymore about Adam. About why he wasn't in school. About what he was hiding. About whether he was okay. About why he was so scared and angry and filled with something I couldn't even understand.

I put the N95 mask on and slipped my phone into my shorts pocket, making my way back outside.

Toward Adam's. Maybe I would knock on his door. Maybe I would lose my nerve. But at least I wouldn't just be sitting here in this quiet house.

Adam might be mad about me showing up. But I was a concerned friend, and how could someone get mad at a concerned friend? Did he even see me as a friend? If not, he'd definitely be mad. So then what did I have to lose? My mind went around and around in circles as I walked toward his house in the hazy air.

I pulled my mask down for a second to take a puff of my inhaler. Suddenly, the wind gusted, dust spackling my face. I stopped in the middle of the road and thought about turning back. But I was now closer to Adam's house than mine, so I picked up speed, pressing the top of the mask down tightly over my nose.

As soon as I reached Adam's house, I knocked on the front door, but no one answered. The wind was howling now, and I wasn't sure that anyone inside could hear my pounding.

Panic began building inside me. The mask couldn't keep every speck of dust out, and I felt my lungs tightening. I had to get inside somewhere, and home was too far away. I spotted the little shed on the other side of the driveway. What if it was locked? I looked around at neighboring houses, but they were farther away. Plus, it was in the middle of the day. People might be at work.

Shielding my face, I made my way to the shed and pushed on the wooden door, jiggling the metal handle. My heart jumped in my chest when it wouldn't open at first. I slammed my whole body against the door, and it finally jerked open. I rushed in and closed the door as tightly as I could, gasping from fear and relief. I bent over for a minute, my hands on my knees, before standing up and taking a puff of my inhaler.

I peered through the dirty shed window at the house, watching for any sign of Adam. Dust seeped in through cracks in the boards and around the window, but there was nothing I could do about that. The rickety shed was still better than outside. My phone vibrated in my pocket, and I pulled it out. It was Dad. I was about to answer when I heard a loud clang. Through the thickening air, I watched the garage door roll upward and a black car pull out. I couldn't see the driver. Adam's uncle? Was Adam with him or was this my chance to talk to Adam without his uncle there?

The car turned down the road as the garage door

began closing. My phone stopped vibrating, but I couldn't call Dad back now. I didn't have a second to lose. The garage would be safer. I burst through the shed door, holding the mask tightly over my mouth with one hand, and bolted for the garage.

I dove to the ground and rolled under the door before it closed. My body must have triggered some kind of sensor, because the door started rolling back up. I jumped to my feet and hit a button mounted on the wall, and the garage door rolled back down again.

I was completely winded from my short sprint, so I sat down next to the door to the house for a few minutes, in the gray light of the closed garage. When my breathing started evening out, I stood and knocked on the door.

No answer.

I knocked again, a little more loudly. Again, no answer.

I stared down at the knob, touching it gently, wondering if it would turn. If I went inside, would I be breaking and entering? I hadn't actually broken anything. So was I just entering? Was that a crime? What was the punishment for entering but not breaking or stealing anything?

I couldn't stay here in this dusty garage. My only options were to call Dad and have him pick me up or go inside. If Dad came and got me, then I'd lose my chance to talk to Adam if he was home. I'd also have some serious explaining to do to Dad.

The knob did turn, and I entered the quiet house. "Adam?" My voice was soft and tentative as I gently closed the door behind me. No answer. "Adam?"

I wandered through the house as my phone buzzed again in my pocket, but I ignored it. The house was neat and clean and plain—totally unremarkable, like the outside. I peeked into a room that looked like it must've been his uncle's. The bed was made and a chair sat in the corner with a man's suit draped across it. The room smelled like cologne.

I peeked in a few other open doorways—a bathroom with some shaving cream and a razor sitting near the sink. A kitchen with just a toaster and blender on the counter. It didn't look or smell like anyone did much cooking in it. Then a laundry room with a few more men's suits hanging on a metal rack.

In my house, the walls were covered with framed photographs of me and Mom and Dad. Of my friends. Of fun times. There were no photographs in this neat and clean and plain house. Finally I came to a closed door.

My phone had been buzzing wildly this entire time. I pulled it out. Three missed calls and all the texts I'd been expecting.

Dad: Why aren't you at school??

Mom: I just got a dust storm warning!!

Dad: Are you OUTSIDE?? Because it looks like you're outside!!

Mom: Why are you outside? THERE IS A DUST STORM COMING! What are you doing?? ANSWER YOUR PHONE RIGHT NOW!!

Dad: If you don't answer, I'm leaving work right now!

They were having a serious fit, so I started to type a reply, but my fingers froze when I heard something. It sounded like...crying? It was coming from inside the closed room. I slipped my phone back into my pocket and knocked gently on the door.

"Adam?" I said his name so softly that it was barely a whisper. I didn't hear any answer, but the crying seemed to quiet as though he'd heard me. I grasped the handle with one unsteady hand and turned it, cracking the door first and then easing it open.

The feeling hit me immediately, like a violent punch to my whole body.

The room was filled with it, stuffed with it, thick and heavy like smog. It was *that* feeling—that dark, dank, dungeon feeling. It was as though the door to the dungeon had been unlocked. The secret bookcase entrance had been emptied. It had been pushed aside. And I felt all of what was in there.

What I'd gotten from Adam before was only wisps compared to what was in this room. This was a whole thunderstorm of it. A raging monsoon. I expected the bedroom walls to bow outward, filled to bursting with it.

That rip in my chest tore open and everything inside me, all that made me human, all that made me who I am, drained out and burned away on the dirty carpeted floor. And then it felt as though someone jammed a hose into the rip and began filling me back up with acid that ate what little was left of me from the inside out until I disappeared completely.

My stomach churned. Bile rose and burned my dust-ravaged throat. I wanted to run away from it, get as far away from it as possible, purge it, scrub it away with a rough steel wool pad like the kind Mom used to clean blackened bits off our pots and pans. I wanted to scour it from my body, even if the scouring was rough and painful and bloody—from my arms and legs and head and chest and all my insides, my mind and heart and stomach—until it was completely gone.

It was shame and pain and anguish and agony and misery and suffering and torment and torture.

Excruciation. E-X-C-R-U-C-I-A-T-I-O-N. Excruciation.

Daylight filtered in through cracks in the dusty, cheap plastic blinds that hung over the only window in the room. It rippled across the walls and floor in skinny lines of light. The whole room looked and smelled and sounded exactly as I felt—all eaten away and dirty and trampled.

Adam was there.

Lying on the bed. Rumpled bed. Covered in

stains. Disgusting stains. In only a T-shirt that barely covered him. Wrinkled T-shirt.

Surrounded by smells. Horrible smells.

Making noises. Whimpering noises.

He had his head buried under a pillow, one arm gripped over top of it so hard that it looked like he could squeeze the pillow in half. Or like he was trying to smother himself.

I had thought my voice would've been eaten away by the acid flowing through me, but then I heard the question coming out. "What is he doing to you?" It sounded as though someone else had asked it, someone whose throat *had* been coated in acid.

At the sound of my voice, Adam tore the pillow away from his head and shot up, pulling the disheveled sheets up to cover the exposed parts of his body— exposed parts that should've only belonged to Adam. Parts I could still feel hands touching. His uncle's hands. Adam could still feel them. And so could I. It was the worst thing I'd ever felt in my entire life.

"What are you doing here?" he demanded. His voice was raw, and his eyes were red and swollen and filled with alarm, cheeks wet with tears, mouth quivering.

A new feeling cut through the heavy excruciation in the room like an arrow shot from a tightly strung bow. Like lightning.

The lightning bolt struck my chest, piercing me all the way to my bones, which shook inside my body. I'd felt fear before, but this was more fear than I knew a person was capable of feeling. The light filtering into the room through the cracks in the flimsy blinds began to dim, growing darker by the second, growing as dark as Adam's face.

I shook where I stood, frozen in place, not sure what to say or do. "Are you okay? I was worried—"

"WHY ARE YOU HERE?" He screamed it this time, hitting me with a powerful gust of anger, so forceful it knocked me back against the wall and sent me tumbling to the floor. A puff of dust floated up from the dirty carpet and filled my lungs. As I pushed to my feet, my head throbbed from being slammed on the wall, and the N95 mask slipped out of my hand. "Adam." I rubbed the back of my head, my voice shaking, my lungs hurting, confusion taking over my mind.

"GET OUT!" A gale of rage hurled me toward the door this time, slamming it shut with the force of my body. The room had dimmed so much that I fumbled for the door handle in the dark, whispering "I'm sorry" over and over again through my tightening lungs.

"GET OUT!" The room was now a swirling cyclone of fury. I finally got the door open and staggered through the opening, feeling my way along the dark hallway with shaking fingers. Spotting the tiniest remnant of light, I moved toward it, slamming my leg on a piece of furniture I couldn't see. Pain shot through my shin as I made my way to a door and pushed my way outside.

Into dust as thick and dark as tar.

chapter 33

Catastrophe.
C-A-T-A-S-T-R-O-P-H-E.
Catastrophe.

I could barely see anything as I stumbled blindly back toward the shed, my lungs closing further with every passing second. But I wandered too long. Where was it? Where was I? In the road now?

I reached into my pocket for the N95 mask, but it wasn't there. Where had it gone? I pulled my shirt up over my face to try to filter some of the dust, but it slipped from my weakening fingers.

Black as night. Nothing but dust. Below me, beside me, above me, behind me, in front of me. I lifted my phone out of my pocket, but the flashlight was no good in this darkness. I tried to call Mom or Dad, but dirt blew in my eyes and blanketed my screen.

Couldn't see or think or breathe. I held the side buttons down to make an emergency call, but the phone slipped out of my hands before the call went through. I scrambled to find it, running my hands over warm, bumpy ground, my eyes stinging, my mind now going into full panic mode.

No time. My airway was now as narrow as a drinking straw. The last thought in my mind before I collapsed was to make sure I wasn't in the road. That was a death sentence. But I had no idea where I was when I hit the ground.

I stared up at the dark, dust-filled sky, my chest burning for air as the black blizzard raged around me. I felt inside my pocket for my inhaler and held it to my mouth, but my fingers no longer had the strength to push downward, and my lungs no longer had the strength to suck in the medicine. The inhaler tumbled out of my hand.

Body cold.

Sweating.

Stars bursting.

Shaking, blurry, dizzy, confusion.

Catastrophe.

C-A-T-A-S-T-R-A...

C-A-S...

C...

Tires squealed. I *was* in the road. About to get run over. But I didn't even have the energy to flinch. Then familiar hands grabbed me—hands that flooded my body with a feeling of terror. Terror that wasn't coming from me. The hands jerked me from the ground and dragged me onto car seats.

My mouth was being pried open by those same hands, the inhaler forced in, the hands pressing my lips down around the opening to seal it.

"Breathe, Avalyn!" Dad screamed.

But all I could muster were weak gasps.

And then we were moving, and I heard Dad's voice frantically yelling at 911. Telling them he needed an ambulance now. Right now. Telling them where we were driving. Telling them he could barely see. That it was like night outside. That his headlights only showed him maybe a few feet of road.

Then the whole world disappeared.

chapter 34

Insidious.
I-N-S-I-D-I-O-U-S.
Insidious.

That was the second time I almost died.

I woke up later that night in a hospital bed with an IV in my arm and a mask on my face, Mom and Dad sitting by my bedside. They gripped my hands in theirs, the dim light creating deep shadows across their faces. I breathed the albuterol deep into my lungs before falling back to sleep.

I dozed on and off throughout the night, but every time I fell asleep, I was back in the room of etched glass, now gasping for every breath. The walls had closed in on me to the point that I could reach out and nearly touch both sides, and I had to duck my head as the glass ceiling lowered.

One time I startled awake, and Mom and Dad weren't sitting by my bed. I spotted them talking softly in the corner. Mom nodded and wiped her eyes as I strained to hear their conversation.

"I just don't see any other choice," she said.

Dad put an arm around her, pulled her to him. "I know." He kissed the top of her head. "I know."

He glanced over at me and saw that my eyes were open. His face brightened. Mom pulled away and turned to me. "Oh, honey," she said, and they both came to stand by my bed, pulling my hands into theirs. "I'm so glad you're awake."

My voice was too weak and hoarse, too muffled for them to understand what I tried to tell them from under my mask.

"Just rest, sweetheart." Dad ran a hand over my head. "Just rest."

I didn't want to sleep. I didn't want to be back in the room of glass. But asleep or awake, it hardly mattered anymore.

I was trapped in that room all the time, and I didn't know how I could ever get out.

The next time I woke up, the mask was gone. My chest hurt in a sore way, like a muscle that had been strained and overused. Even though it was painful to suck in a deep breath, my lungs felt more open. I turned my head and found Dad reclined in a chair next to my bed, dozing.

"Where's Mom?" I croaked.

His eyes shot open, and he rubbed them. Then they moved to me.

"Where's Mom?"

He sat up and leaned in close, his elbows on his knees. "She just went to get you some clean clothes. They're probably going to discharge you at some point today."

My eyes started filling and my lips trembled. I had so much to tell him but didn't know where to begin.

"Oh, honey." He grabbed my hand. "It's going to be okay. You'll be okay."

I shook my head. "I don't want to move. I know that's what you were talking about last night. But I don't want to move again. I don't want to leave my friends."

And I couldn't leave Adam like this. Not like this.

Dad released my hand, letting out an exhausted breath and rubbing his eyes. "We can talk about that later."

"No, I want to talk about it now."

"We may not have a choice, Avalyn. We came here to protect you, but now this place is hurting you."

"But this isn't normal," I said. "The dust will stop."

"We don't know that. It's getting hotter and drier here all the time. This may be the way it is from now on."

"No, it's not. I *know* it's not."

Dad gave me a sad smile. "You do, do you?"

A tear broke loose and rolled down my cheek. "I'm going to make it stop. I'm not going to be the elephant fish anymore. I'm going to make it all stop."

Dad drew his eyebrows together and tilted his head back. Everything I'd just said probably sounded like complete nonsense to him. He slowly shook his head. "Avalyn, I don't—"

"I mean..." What did I mean? How was I going to stop the dust? How could I do anything about what was happening? "I don't mean anything." I sniffled. "My mind is all fuzzy."

We sat there quietly for a long time, Dad running a hand over my forehead, looking like he hadn't slept in a month. "Why were you outside in the dust storm, honey?" he finally asked. "Why did you leave school? Where were you going?"

How could I explain this to him? I could hear myself saying the words—*I think I know what's causing the dust. It's that boy, Adam. He brought it with him, and so when I left school because jerks poured dirt on me, I decided to go talk to him. But I made him so upset by walking in on something he didn't want me to see, that it caused a massive dust storm.* Mom and Dad would probably move me to the psych ward.

"I was worried about someone," I whispered.

Dad's face filled with concern. "Who?"

But again, I wasn't sure how I could explain it all. Science and Pavel Belsky and Dillon and the elephant fish—nothing could explain it. The world didn't make sense anymore. I slowly shook my head, tears running down my cheeks.

"You don't want to tell me?"

"It's not that." What was it? I was having trouble

262

thinking clearly. Processing all of it. I said the first thing that came to my mind. "Do you know what happens when people hurt each other?"

Dad's eyes widened. He opened his mouth, but then he closed it. Opened it again. Closed it. Then finally spoke. "What, Avalyn?"

"When people hurt each other," I repeated, my voice quavering, "the hurt doesn't stop at one person. The person who got hurt hurts someone else because of how bad they feel. And that person hurts someone else. And it spreads everywhere." Dad picked up a corner of my bedsheet and dabbed the tears from my cheeks with it. "It's... It's..." Insidious. I-N-S-I-D-I-O-U-S. Insidious. "Like dust in a dust storm," I whispered.

Dad sat there a long time, wiping my cheeks and pushing my hair back from my face, like he was trying to think of how to respond to what I'd said. "Yes, that can happen," he finally said. "Unless someone decides to stop the cycle."

My mouth trembled. "But what can one person even do?" I squeezed the hospital sheets in my fists. "It feels like trying to fight a dust storm with a feather duster."

He gripped my hand in his. "Yes, you're only one person, but you know what we've always told you. A single voice can be powerful. *Your* voice can be powerful. You are definitely not powerless, Avalyn."

"Impuissant," I uttered.

He smiled and kissed my hand. "Right. You're not impuissant. And anyway, just because someone's been hurt doesn't mean they're destined to hurt others."

"But they do."

Dad nodded. "Sometimes. But it's not all hopeless. People break the cycle of hurt all the time."

"How? How does someone stop it?"

Dad leaned in. "Sweetheart," he said softly, "do you know someone who's being hurt? Is it the person you were worried about?"

I nodded, the tears spilling down my cheeks and onto the hospital sheets still clenched in my fists. "Maybe."

"Is this a child who's being hurt? A child at school?" I nodded. "Is it an adult who's hurting them?"

Again, I nodded.

Dad sighed, rubbing his eyes and forehead. "Then, honey, you need to say something. Tell someone what you know. You can tell me right now if you want to, and I'll figure out what to do about it."

But would people believe me? Would they believe Adam? Would Adam tell the truth? I didn't have any proof of what I'd seen. Of what I'd felt. Of what I knew.

Just the dust. All I had was dust.

"I'm . . . I want to talk to my friend first, I think."

Dad frowned. "It's possible this friend won't want you to tell. They could be protecting the adult who's hurting them. Maybe they've been threatened if they tell. Or maybe they feel ashamed."

Ashamed. I remembered the feeling in Adam's room, and I chased away the memory, never wanting to feel that way again. "I don't think they want anyone to know."

"So, will talking to them help, then? What will you do when they tell you to keep it a secret?"

I shook my head. "I don't know. I'm worried they'll hate me if I tell anyone about what I know because I think you're right about them feeling ashamed." I didn't think anything. I knew Dad was right. The shame I'd felt in that room had etched a mark into me forever. As much as I wanted to forget, I never would.

"Speaking up may ruin your friendship with this person, Avalyn. Sometimes speaking up will cause you to lose a whole lot more than that. But what does your silence cost?"

Adam. Dillon. Nan. Me. Everyone.

Dad leaned in, squeezing my hands in his so firmly it almost hurt. "Avalyn." His face was as gravely serious as I'd ever seen. "If you know someone is being hurt, then no matter what your friend wants—even if you think they won't want to be friends with you anymore—no matter what may happen, you have to take that risk. It's not even a choice, honey. You *have* to tell."

chapter 35

Ebullient.
E-B-U-L-L-I-E-N-T.
Ebullient.

It was good to be home from the hospital with no pressure to go back to school. I still felt weak and tired, so I spent the next day resting in bed, reading my X-Men comics and staring at my window, so foggy and etched now from the black blizzard, I could barely make out blurry shapes outside. And the cloudier my window got, the more it felt like the walls in the room of cloudy glass were closing in on me. The less oxygen was left in the room to breathe. The more I suffocated. I was in the room all the time now, whether asleep or awake. I was always in that room.

There was a knock on my door. "Come in."

Dad cracked the door. "Someone's here to see you."

I stood up from the bed, my heart thumping, my hands twisting together. Would Adam have come to check on me after what happened? "He is?"

Nan and Dillon poked their heads into the room, under Dad's arm. When they saw me, Dillon said, "Hello, marvelous person."

I tried to say it back, but the words caught in my throat. Pressure built behind my eyes.

They both smiled hugely and ran my way, wrapping their arms around me, the three of us falling back onto the bed in a tangled, laughing mess. My whole body filled with bubbles, bursting and popping and fizzing and sizzling. I felt effervescent. Ebullient. E-B-U-L-L-I-E-N-T. Ebullient.

"I want to kill you for scaring us like that," Dillon said, and I realized he was actually crying, not laughing.

Nan sniffled. "If you had died, I'd have really killed you."

We all started giggling as Dad gently shut the door. I pushed my friends off me, and the three of us sat side by side on the bed. Dillon wiped his eyes, and I put an arm around him. "I'm okay." Then I leaned my head on his shoulder. "Are...you okay?"

I knew he knew what I meant because I suddenly felt the bra tied around my chest. I squeezed him tighter to me.

"Yeah," he said softly. "I'm getting there."

"What happened?" asked Nan. "Your parents said you got caught in a dust storm. That you were down the street and you fainted and your dad had to find you and you were just lying there in the street and—"

"Yes." I didn't need her to replay the whole awful event for me.

"But why?" she asked. "How?"

I swallowed. "You know that kid, Adam?"

They looked at each other before looking at me. "Yeah," said Nan.

"I think...I think something very bad is happening to him."

"Avalyn," said Dillon. "What does that have to do with you getting caught in a dust storm?"

"Everything. It has everything to do with it."

They both looked at me with questioning eyes.

"If I tell you guys something, you're going to think I'm nuts."

"We'd never think that," said Nan.

"Never," added Dillon.

I took a deep breath. Maybe it was time to finally trust someone with this, and I couldn't think of anyone better than my two best friends. "You know how I've been sort of obsessing over telepathy and telekinesis and all that?"

"Of course," said Dillon.

"Well...this is why." I waited a moment, gathering my thoughts, preparing my words. Then I told them what I believed about Adam and the dust. And even though I knew they had their doubts, even though they were skeptical, especially Dillon, they listened to what I had to say. They asked questions and heard my reasons for believing what I did. They acknowledged every word because the words were important to me. And they didn't try to talk me out of any of it.

Because they were marvelous people.

chapter 36

Nescient.
N-E-S-C-I-E-N-T.
Nescient.

I asked Mom to drive me to school my first day back so I wouldn't accidentally run into Adam on the way there. She was, of course, more than happy to take me, still being all shaken up herself from my ordeal.

What would I say to Adam when I saw him? Maybe he'd never want to talk to me again. Maybe he hated me. It had felt like he hated me that day in that…that awful room.

Mom stopped the car in front of school and put it in park. Then she turned to me. "Honey."

I stared down at my lap, playing with the N95

mask she'd given me, twisting it until one of the ear loops snapped. I startled a little at what I'd done and quickly folded the mask into my hands so Mom wouldn't see.

"I know this is hard," she said. "But you can do this, Avalyn."

I swallowed. "Mom, I don't want to talk about this anymore."

"I know you don't. I know you're not ready to tell us exactly what happened or who you're talking about. And I'll tell you something else I know." She reached over and put her hand gently on my chin, turning my head so I was looking at her. "You're a good person."

I turned my head out of her grip. Because I didn't want her to see the look on my face—the look that said I wasn't sure I agreed with her. I thought of Empath, of Rogue, of Magneto. All villains who thought they were actually heroes, and the characters I identified more with than anyone else.

Her face was stern. "Good people don't stand by and say nothing while others get hurt."

Maybe I was a villain and was completely nescient about it like the rest of them. N-E-S-C-I-E-N-T. Nescient.

I got out of the car and shut the door. I walked across campus to my first class, not even looking for Nan or Dillon, scared of running into Adam. I just wanted to get to class and zone out for the next hour.

Valerie snickered at me as I tossed my backpack onto my desk and sat down, trying not to look at her. "Where have you been?" she asked. "Did it take you all week to get the dirt out of your hair?"

I pretended that I didn't hear her, biting the inside of my lip so hard it bled, willing class to begin so she would have to shut up. Always waiting for something else to happen. For someone else to say something. For someone else to come to my rescue. Always waiting, as the glass closed in.

I flipped through the sample yearbook, looking for the slightest typo or mistake. Ms. Lund said she couldn't have asked for a better proofreader than I was, but I could barely force myself to focus on misspellings or grammatical errors.

There were a lot of pictures in the yearbook I hadn't seen before—pictures Adam had taken. "Have you seen Adam lately?" I asked Ms. Lund.

"No," she said from behind the counter, where she was labeling a new stack of books. "He hasn't been around since he brought me his last batch of pictures. Let's see...that had to be over a week ago now."

"Did he seem...okay to you?"

She frowned. "No, he seemed upset. But he's a tough book to read, you know?"

I nodded. Yes, I did know. I knew far too much. I shuddered and tried to turn my attention back to the yearbook.

"Are *you* okay, Avalyn?"

I stared down at the page: the student poll. "I hate pages ninety-one and ninety-two. I *hate* them."

She set the book she'd been holding down and tilted her head. "Those are some strong words. What's on those pages?"

"The student poll," I said. "And I hate the categories."

Ms. Lund got up and walked to me, hovering over the sample pages. "What's wrong with them?"

I read them off. "Most popular, best dressed, best dancer. It's all a bunch of stupid, superficial stuff."

Ms. Lund stared down at me. "You know something, Avalyn? I think you're right."

"Then why do we even have it?"

She shrugged. "We've always had the student poll in the yearbook. It's what everyone expects."

I glared at the pages. "Everyone wants things to stay the same. But just because we've always had the student poll in the yearbook and it's what people expect doesn't mean it's what's best. That seems really nescient if you ask me."

Ms. Lund smiled down at me. "That *is* a nescient way of thinking, Avalyn. So what would you suggest, then?"

I tapped my finger on the yearbook. "Maybe we should get rid of it."

"I think that would make some people unhappy," she said. "They look forward to seeing it."

"Not everyone looks forward to it."

"Well"—Ms. Lund scratched her scalp with the tip of her pencil—"why don't you think on it? I'll think on it, too. Maybe we can come up with a good solution if we put our heads together."

When the fifth-period bell rang, I said goodbye to Ms. Lund and left the media center with Nan and Dillon.

"I hate the student poll, too," said Nan.

I slipped my arm through hers. "I didn't know you were spying on our conversation."

"Kind of hard to avoid, since we were the only people in there," said Dillon. "And I agree. It's always the same stupid people who win everything."

"Maybe you should make it something silly," said Nan. "Like 'Most Vans' or 'Coolest Tapestry'"

I smiled. "Then you guys would finally have a chance."

"I don't want to be in the poll," said Dillon. "I'd just like to see someone else win for a change."

I left my friends and started making my way to the other side of campus, thinking about the student poll instead of Adam for the first time all day.

Of course, the moment he left my mind was when he finally showed up.

chapter 37

Maelstrom.
M-A-E-L-S-T-R-O-M.
Maelstrom.

He caught my eye from about fifty feet away, across the open brown field at the center of school that used to be green before the dust blanketed it and killed the grass. I wished we could speak through the air. Like electricity. I would tell him I was sorry for everything. Sorry that this was happening to him. Sorry I walked in and saw something he didn't want me to see. Felt something he didn't want me to feel. He would tell me he was sorry that he screamed at me and sent me out into the dust. Was he sorry? Maybe not. Maybe I just really wanted him to be.

But whatever he was thinking, he needed to understand that I couldn't unsee, unhear, unfeel all that I had seen, heard, and felt. Nor did I know how much longer I could unspeak it. The words were starting to burn, etching my insides, making everything within me raw and painful.

Despite all the students bustling around, trying to get to fifth period on time, I was totally focused on Adam. I'd blurred the rest of the world out. So I didn't notice Emma sneaking up behind him. Didn't notice the look on her face. Didn't notice her reach out toward him—until she gripped his pants from behind.

This time I found my voice and started moving toward them. "NO!"

But I was too late. She pulled them down. And his underwear came down with them.

He stood there frozen, all of him on display. Kids snickered. Kids gasped. Kids turned away, covered their eyes. Kids shouted terrible things. It was as though time had stopped for me and Adam while it continued to move forward for everyone else.

After what felt like decades, Adam bent down,

gripped his sweats, and pulled them up in fists clenched so white I could see their pale color from where I stood on the other side of the field.

Electricity began building. It crackled all around me, getting louder and louder, as though the air were filled with a growing fire, burning bigger and hotter. My hair rose and hovered over my head while my body hummed and limbs tingled.

The wind started blowing.

The air thickened.

The sky darkened.

Someone screamed.

In the distance behind Adam, a black wall of dust unlike anything I'd ever seen barreled toward us. It was somehow higher than the sun, wider than the sky, bigger than the earth, capable of enveloping the whole universe. The wind carrying it hit me so hard that I was forced to take baby steps backward to keep from falling over.

Everyone around us ran, screaming, from the black wall rolling toward our school like a tsunami made of pitch. They slammed through doors, climbing over one another to get inside, to safety. But Adam stood alone across from me, eyes squeezed shut, pale skin now bright red, black sweats still clenched in his balled fists.

This wall of dust would suffocate everything in its path.

The sun dimmed like a sudden eclipse, and I had a choice to make: run and hide and leave Adam here to suffer alone and out of control. Or go to him.

I moved toward Adam, the wind growing stronger, pushing me back. I fought against it, my body angled forward. I had to reach Adam before the wall of dust reached me. I slowly closed the distance between us with labored steps that slid backward on the sandy grass.

There was no time for questions now. No time for explanations. No time for doubt. I had to believe what I could do. If it was possible for Adam to be Wind Dancer in this strange world, then maybe I could really be Rogue.

I finally made it to Adam as the black wall hovered just behind him, so high I couldn't see its top. He still had his eyes and fists clenched, his whole body shaking violently.

Then he opened his red-rimmed, pale eyes and

saw me. Knew me. And in those glistening, tear-filled eyes, there was more pain than I knew could be contained within a single person. But not just pain. There was also pleading.

Adam unclenched one of his fists and reached out to me, as though he were hanging from a cliff by a single fingertip. As though he were drowning.

I couldn't have heard anything he said, but he didn't have to say anything. It was all there in his eyes: *Please. Help. Please.*

I grabbed Adam's hand.

An enormous shock exploded between us, a shock so bright and hot it burned my skin. It took all my strength not to pull away from him, especially when I began absorbing what was inside him.

And what I began absorbing wasn't just hate. It wasn't just anger and fury and fear. It wasn't just shame.

It was a tornado. A cyclone. A maelstrom of pain. A hurricane of rage, gusting inside me, creating a pressure so intense that every single inch of my body felt pushed outward like the walls of that terrible bedroom where I'd found Adam.

My ears popped, and wind seeped out of every

crack it could find—out of my pursed lips and nose and even the corners of my eyes, making them whistle. I gathered every bit of power within me to hold it in. I would need all of it.

Finally, when there seemed to be nothing left and I felt I couldn't hold another wisp of it, I pulled my hand away.

I turned and raised my trembling arms, planted my feet firmly, and held my hands up—palms out, fingers splayed—to the enormous wall of dust, as though I was ordering it to stop.

Then I opened my mouth and released the hurricane, aiming it at the wall. I screamed it out, my feet sliding, leaving parallel tracks in the sand. I dug my feet deeper into the sandy grass, leaned forward, and continued howling it out, breathing it out, and finally gasping out.

Every breath inside me.

Because as my parents always told me, breath is powerful. What I choose to do with my breath can change the world. Or maybe just one person's world.

When my arms became limp and my knees weakened and I could no longer stand strong, the remaining force of what was left inside me blew me backward, onto my back on the sand-cushioned grass.

The last whisper of wind was forced out of my lungs as I hit the ground, and everything turned to black.

chapter 38

Veritas.
V-E-R-I-T-A-S.
Veritas.

My eyelids fluttered open, a checkerboard of white ceiling tiles and air-conditioning vents and fluorescent lights gradually coming into view. I shifted and grunted where I lay—on a mattress somewhere. Someone was speaking softly.

"Yes, she's breathing okay," the voice said. "No, I'm not sure what happened. I guess she fainted outside." A long silence. "Another student carried her in here."

It was Ms. Imani. She must've been talking to Mom or Dad. I pushed myself up on my elbows and found her standing over her desk, fiddling with a pen, the phone pressed to her ear. She looked up at me and smiled. "She's up now. You want to talk to her?"

Ms. Imani brought me the phone, pressing it to my ear. I sat up fully so I could take it from her. "Hello?" I said. My voice sounded like it had been sandblasted.

"Are you okay?" Mom said, her voice quick and high-pitched with anxiety.

I gazed out the nearest window, searching for the black wall of dust. "Yes." The air was clear, the sky blue, the sun shining. "I think I got dizzy." With my free hand, I grasped several strands of hair and held them in front of my face so I could inspect them, but they were still plain brown. No white streak.

"Are you losing your voice?" Mom said, then before I could answer, added, "We knew it was too soon for you to go back to school. I'm leaving work to get you now."

I pushed my hair back from my face as a cactus wren landed on the windowsill and pecked at a couple of bugs. "You don't have to," I mumbled. I reached out and touched the metal window frame, but there was no spark of static electricity.

"Avalyn, you fainted. You need to come home. I'll be there in twenty."

I withdrew my hand from the windowsill, and the cactus wren flew away. "Okay," I said, my gritty, hoarse voice apparently the only evidence left of the giant wall of dust.

"Be there soon. Love you."

"Love you, too." I handed the phone back to Ms. Imani, who carried it to the desk and set it down on the receiver.

She sat next to me on the bed, and I watched the window a minute longer before turning my head to her. She was staring at me with caring eyes and open ears. Waiting to hear what I had to say. When I said nothing, she asked, "What happened out there, Avalyn? Some kids said a big dust storm was coming, but the wind must've died."

I sat there, still unspeaking—all those feelings and words buried deep inside the room of foggy glass. Words screaming and crying, putting pressure on my head and heart and the backs of my eyes, pushing tears out. Like the hurricane. But this wasn't a hurricane of rage and anger and hurt. This was a hurricane of need—of needing to be let out. Out of the room of etched foggy glass.

Ms. Imani continued staring at me with those expectant eyes. "Is everything okay, Avalyn?"

I shook my head slowly and let the tears stream down my cheeks. And Ms. Imani continued to watch me. Patiently waiting. No hurry. She seemed to sense something important was all pent up inside me. Something that needed to be released but couldn't be forced out too quickly. It had to be let out gently, like air out of a balloon. Just a little at a time or the balloon would slip out of my hands and fly wildly out of control.

Letters were forming in my chest, filling my previously empty cavity. Letters that needed to be let out.

V validated.

E endured.

R repaired.

I informed.

T tended.

A amended.

S set free.

I finally opened my mouth, just a crack, to let the words seep out. At first, they were a tentative, whispering tendril of what I'd seen. But soon they turned into a building breeze of what I believed, which quickly became a whooshing wind of truth.

"I told her everything." Mom, Dad, and I sat on the couch together, me in the middle. "I told her everything I just told you."

I'd told them about Adam. About what I saw at his house. About what Emma had done to him at school. About what her friends had done to Dillon. About that whole terrible day, from the bucket of dirt on my head to collapsing in the street.

Mom and Dad hugged me and cried. For Adam. For Dillon. For me and what had happened. For what I'd seen. For what I knew. And I thought, if it felt this bad just knowing what Adam's uncle was doing to him, how bad must it have been for Adam....

But I wasn't the only one who knew anymore. Now Ms. Imani knew. Mom and Dad knew. The police would know, too. And Adam would figure out that it was me. That I was the one who told about him and his uncle. Whatever happened now, he'd know it was me who caused it.

But I didn't tell them about the wind and the dust and the electricity and the hurricane. I didn't tell them that Adam and I were real X-Men.

chapter 39

Vicissitude.
V-I-C-I-S-S-I-T-U-D-E.
Vicissitude.

I knew the moment they took Adam away. I didn't see it happen. I didn't hear it happen. I felt it happen. The static electricity that had been building in the air again shut off like a switch had been flipped, and the dust settled. At least the dust *outside*.

My mind ran and ran with questions. What had I done? Had I done good? Had I caused him more hurt? Where would they take him? Did he have somewhere else to go? Did he hate me?

All that had happened left something worse than emptiness inside me. Worse because it wasn't just empty—it was now filled with unanswered questions. And dust. There was dust in there, too.

The evening before the spelling bee, I took a long walk through the desert. Just because I could. The air was clear, warm, and still, and Mom and Dad didn't even have me triple-check my inhaler or Big Brother or N95 mask before I left. They just let me go. Well, except for telling me to watch the ground for rattlesnakes. And scorpions. And cactus needles.

I tried not to think about Adam. Tried not to think of where he'd gone or how he was doing or what had happened to him. I tried to think of the spelling bee instead, so I spelled out words.

Concomitant. C-O-N-C-O-M-I-T-A-N-T. Concomitant.

Unpropitious. U-N-P-R-O-P-I-T-I-O-U-S. Unpropitious.

Vicissitude. V-I-C-I-S-S-I-T-U-D-E. Vicissitude.

Necessary. N-E-C-E-S-S-A-R-Y. Necessary.

I walked by brittlebushes and their blooms, already dried up. The few desert wildflowers we'd had this year had already become withered brown twigs that disintegrated when I ran my shoe over them. A couple of quail pecked at the ground nearby, and again I looked for babies but didn't spot any. Maybe the drought had been too much for them—not enough food and fewer plants for hiding. I wondered if the coming summer would be as dry as the last summer had been and if the monsoons would bring dust storms. Normal dust storms. Would the saguaro outside my window survive?

I found myself nearing Adam's house, and I tried not to look at it as I passed by. But then I was standing in front of it, thinking of things I didn't want to think about. Adam wasn't in there. His uncle wasn't in there either. The house seemed dead, a carcass or a corpse left over from some violent, bloody event.

Would I be able to feel what was left inside that house if I were to enter it uninvited again? Had the shame, thick as sludge, soaked into the carpet? Had the pain, heavy as smoke, saturated the walls? I didn't want to know. I never wanted to feel that way again. And I hoped Adam would stop feeling that way someday, but I knew feelings that strong couldn't possibly dissolve like salt in water.

But maybe their sharp edges, jagged enough to wear and whittle a person down to nothing more than slivers and splinters and shavings, could be sanded smooth. Like sea glass. The glass never wears away completely, but every bit of it becomes etched and cloudy. Over a long time, the edges of the glass soften, less able to cut skin and draw blood. And as that happens, maybe those slivers and splinters and shavings are able to bond back together.

I needed to believe they could become whole again.

chapter 40

Conscious.
C-O-N-S-C-I-O-U-S.
Conscious.

One by one, the winners of the classroom bees went up to spell their words. And one by one, they eventually misspelled and lost their seat on the stage. All except me and Daniel Garza. We sat side by side and couldn't help smiling at each other as the third-to-last person misspelled *ichthyosaurus*.

I scanned the audience and found Nan and Dillon. They made silly faces to try to get me to crack up onstage, and I bit my lip to keep from giggling. They knew I would win this time. I never, *ever* misspelled.

My eyes moved to Valerie sitting not far from them.

Her searing glare burned away any and all giggling urges, replacing them with a sickness in my stomach. I quickly looked away and made an effort not to look at her or any of the Meanie Butt Band, who were clearly super unhappy about having to sit through this.

They hated me now just as much as they hated Dillon. The Meanie Butt Band had been given detention for what they did to Adam, Dillon, and me. Dr. Delgado even threatened them with expulsion if they ever physically bullied anyone again. But things still didn't feel right.

Daniel's name was called. He took a deep breath and gave me one last *Wish me luck* look before walking to the microphone.

Mr. Griffin read from the card in his hands. "Daniel, your word is *iconoclast.*"

Iconoclast wasn't a hard word, and I wondered how long this could go on with just the two of us. We could be up here forever.

Daniel took another deep breath and adjusted the microphone. "May I get a definition, please?"

"Sure." Mr. Griffin looked back down at his card. "An iconoclast is a person who criticizes or attacks a society's accepted beliefs or customs."

Daniel cleared his throat. "Can you use it in a sentence, please?"

Mr. Griffin nodded. "She was a rebel, a dissenter, an *iconoclast*, who protested the long-accepted injustices associated with her society's traditions."

Daniel smiled. "Iconoclast. I…C…O…N…O… C…L…A…S…T. Iconoclast."

The word rang in my head. *Iconoclast. Iconoclast. Iconoclast.*

Critic, skeptic, heretic.

Mr. Griffin turned to me. "Avalyn?"

I stood and walked to the podium. *Iconoclast. Iconoclast. Iconoclast.*

Dissenter, protester, disrupter.

With slightly shaking fingers, I adjusted the microphone as Daniel had, so it was nearly touching my lips. *Iconoclast, iconoclast, iconoclast.*

Renegade, rebel, revolutionary.

"Avalyn"—Mr. Griffin's loud voice startled me— "your word is *subterranean.*"

Ms. Lund raised the green card indicating my two minutes had begun. I breathed in and out. *Slow it down. In and out.* I fidgeted with the microphone again even though it was already at the right height.

Subterranean was an easy word. *Subterranean* exists under the earth's surface, where I wanted to burrow and dig and live whenever I looked out at the crowd and saw Emma's face all scrunched up in disgust, Bryden rolling his eyes like this was the biggest waste of his time. When I thought of myself ignoring it and keeping quiet. Always keeping quiet.

I zeroed in on Nan and Dillon. They were subtly holding their fists up and smiling, as though to say, *Keep going. Keep fighting.*

Keep fighting.

When was I ever fighting in the first place?

The weight of everything crushed me up on the stage. I could feel all of it at once—the dirt that had been poured on my head, Adam's pants being pulled down, the bra tied around Dillon's chest. I felt it all.

And I suddenly realized that everyone in that whole school, even the yawners, even the ones who'd been rolling their eyes—every single one of them had to sit there and listen to me right now. All of them wondering if I was going to fail. Some of them hoping I would fail. Waiting to make fun of me for failing. For even spelling in the first place.

But I was the one with the microphone. And they

couldn't say anything back. Couldn't shout *Wheezer* at me without getting in trouble. When would this ever happen again?

Two minutes. Two minutes was all I had. Two minutes is about thirty-two breaths. And a whole lot of letters.

"S," I said, my voice quavering.

Everyone looking at me. Waiting. Listening.

I was trapped in that foggy, sandblasted-glass room. Despite having told all that I had, I was still in that dim, foggy, suffocating room, the oxygen being depleted every single day. I was still choking, unable to see clearly, unable to breathe fresh air. The glass walls were now close enough that I could reach out both arms and press my palms against opposite walls, elbows bent. I felt the glass for the first time and realized it was rough. It wasn't just that I was running out of oxygen, that I would soon be smothered by the glass walls. The dust storm wasn't outside the room. It was *inside* the room with me, etching the glass from the inside.

Face like fire and eyes burning. Hands and legs shaking. Vision going blurry. Head pounding, stomach cramping, heart hurting.

I looked down and spotted a sledgehammer on the floor of the glass room with me. I finally saw the way out. I could get myself out. No one was going to come and let me out. It was on *me.*

For the first time in a long time, I felt totally conscious. C-O-N-S-C-I-O-U-S. Conscious. I was waking up from this nightmare.

My breathing sped up with fear and anxiety and excitement and nerves. Because I knew I was about to blow the spelling bee.

On purpose.

chapter 41

Iconoclast.
I-C-O-N-O-C-L-A-S-T.
Iconoclast.

I turned to Mr. Griffin. "May I start over, please?" I asked, barely above a whisper.

"Yes, but you must use the same letters you've already used."

I turned back to the school. To my classmates. I picked up the sledgehammer from the floor of the glass room. I held it, gripping it tightly in both hands, and aimed it at the glass ceiling above me. Up until today, *subterranean* had always been spelled S-U-B-T-E-R-R-A-N-E-A-N. But today, I swung the sledgehammer upward and spelled it "S...T...O...P."

The glass ceiling shattered.

Mr. Griffin gave me a bewildered look. He lifted his card to study the word, like he may have somehow misread or misremembered it. He pushed his glasses up his nose. "Avalyn, I'm sorry, but—"

"I'm not done spelling," I blurted out. "I'm not done."

I turned back to my school, the sledgehammer still held firmly in my hands. I wasn't done.

Spelling is my superpower.

"S...T...O...P," I said again, my voice and hands trembling. "B...U...L...L...Y...I...N...G." I paused, sucked in a difficult breath, hoped my airway stayed open long enough to finish this spelling bee. I held the sledgehammer over my head now that the glass ceiling was gone. "U...S." I swung it again, busting a foggy glass wall to pieces.

Mr. Griffin scowled at me. "That's incorrect."

"I'm still not done."

"I think you are."

"I'm not," I insisted, looking to Ms. Lund for help,

her eyes wide with surprise, the yellow and red cards held in her lap.

She stood and cleared her throat. "Avalyn has two minutes to spell. As long as she's still spelling, she can continue."

"This is not the right time for this," said Mr. Griffin.

Dr. Delgado rose from his seat next to Ms. Lund. "Avalyn has earned her two minutes up on that stage," he said to Mr. Griffin. "And you've just wasted a good portion of that." Then he looked at Ms. Lund. "Please add back the time that was wasted so Avalyn has her full two minutes." He nodded at me. "Please proceed, Avalyn."

I was so grateful for Dr. Delgado in that moment. Because I knew, right then, that he really did care about us. It wasn't just a show. It wasn't just to appease the parents. I could *feel* his concern. And that gave me more power.

I gripped my hands together, squeezing them as hard as I could to stop the trembling, as though they were really and truly holding on to that sledge-hammer with every bit of strength I had.

Spelling can't be a superpower.

I spelled more quickly this time. "S-T-O-P."

"A-B-U-S-I-N-G."

"U-S." I swung the sledgehammer and smashed another wall.

Why not?

"S-T-O-P."

"A-S-S-A-U-L-T-I-N-G."

"U-S."

Ms. Lund raised the yellow card, indicating I still had forty-five seconds.

Superheroes use their superpowers for good.

When my legs felt like they might buckle, like I couldn't bear the weight of the sledgehammer anymore, couldn't lift it over my head, I focused on Nan and Dillon, on their two small figures in the crowd. Their eyes were so big that I could see the whites gleaming. They gripped hands, but across the sea of kids, it felt as though they were gripping me. Gripping the sledgehammer with me. Lifting it up. Lifting *me* up. As I looked over the auditorium, I realized a lot of hands were on the handle of that sledgehammer.

"S-T-O-P."

"H-A-R-A-S-S-I-N-G."

"U-S." I took a deep breath as I smashed another glass wall.

Ms. Lund still hadn't raised the red card, and it was as though suddenly, with only a look, I could pull emotion from people, as though my own power was growing with every letter. I could see everything I needed in Ms. Lund's eyes.

"S-T-O-P."

"H-U-R-T-I-N-G."

"U-S." I took one last deep breath.

"S." Every. "T." Letter. "O." Was. "P." Painful, but I pushed out that final *P*, and with the last bit of strength I had, I raised the sledgehammer and smashed the final wall.

There I stood, up on that stage, in the open air. I wiped the last of the dust from eyes and expelled the last of it from my lungs. Standing in all that clear fresh air, shattered glass at my feet, was overwhelming. Dizzying. It made me lightheaded, but I stayed standing.

Ms. Lund finally raised the red card. She stared at me, the card gripped in her hand. Then she stood and, wiping her cheek with her free hand, slowly turned until she was facing the crowd of students. She raised the red card high above her head. Raising it to the whole school. Sending a message to everyone in the entire building.

It was time to stop.

chapter 42

Amelioration.
A-M-E-L-I-O-R-A-T-I-O-N.
Amelioration.

"Guess what I got for an early birthday present?" Nan asked. The three of us were sitting on a bench outside together, waiting for the first bell of the day to ring. It was getting pretty hot, but it wasn't unbearable yet, and the air was clear again. I knew I should've been relieved that the dust had gone away and hadn't come back, but it just reminded me that Adam was gone, too, and that I hadn't heard from him. I had no idea where he'd gone or what was happening to him. If he was okay. If he was angry with me. If he hated me.

"What?" Dillon asked.

Nan reached into the front pocket on her backpack and pulled out some papers. "Fan Fusion tickets! And this time, Avalyn, I got three tickets." She handed one to Dillon and one to me.

Dillon excitedly turned his ticket over and over in his hands. "I can't wait. I already know what I'm going to dress up as."

"Oh, let us guess!" Nan squealed.

"Goldballs!" I blurted out, and the three of us cracked up.

Dillon shook his head. "No way. I do *not* lay eggs, not even gold ones."

"Spider-Man?" Nan said.

Dillon frowned at her. "Why would I go as Spider-Man?"

"Because he's a science nerd," she said.

Dillon rolled his eyes. "Like all science nerds are the same. We're individuals, I'll have you know."

"I know," I said. "Pavel Belsky."

Dillon beamed. "Of course."

"Oh, like he's not a science nerd," scoffed Nan.

"Not just a regular old science nerd. He's the *king* of science nerds."

"No one will even know who you are," said Nan. "He just wears T-shirts and looks totally normal."

"You two will know. And that's all that matters."

Nan threw her long dark hair back. "Well, I'm going to go as Bastille."

Dillon and I stared at her. "Who even is that?" Dillon finally asked.

"Bastille Vianitelle Dartmoor from *Alcatraz vs. the Evil Librarians*. Duh! She is a knight of Crystallia and wears the coolest crystal armor and carries a crystal sword." Nan made a motion like she was chopping us both in half with a sword. "I've already been researching how to make the costume."

"How do you make a crystal costume?" I asked.

"Like, plastic wrap and stuff. How about you, Avalyn? What are you going to be?"

I didn't even have to think about it. "WordGirl."

Dillon nodded. "Nice choice."

"Yeah, Avalyn," said Nan. "That is so you."

"Thanks." My cheeks warmed and not just from the desert heat. Sometimes it was still hard to be yourself, even in front of the people who knew you the best.

Nan clapped her hands excitedly. "Oh! We also need to talk about my party."

"Is the pool going to be done on time?" I asked.

"The builder guys promised it will be."

Dillon and I looked at each other and pumped our fists. "Yes," we both said. No more lounging on blazing-hot fake grass and spraying one another with the hose. This was going to be life changing this summer.

The bell rang, and we went our separate ways for our first class of the day. A knot twisted in my stomach—we'd be doing the student poll this morning. I tried to think of my WordGirl costume as I sat down quietly and waited for the poll to be handed out. I would need red and yellow fabric, or maybe I could use a red hoodie and red leggings. Maybe Dad could help me with the belt. Red boots? No, I'd just wear black boots, or maybe—

"What the heck is this?" Emma said, interrupting my focus. I'd been concentrating so hard that I hadn't realized the poll was sitting on my desk. "Why are we doing another poll?"

Mr. Sheffield picked up the poll and read it. "I guess someone decided to make some changes this year." He winked at me.

"Why are these all different?" Emma whined. "Where's best dressed?"

"You're responsible for this," Valerie sneered at me. "Aren't you? Only you could come up with something as stupid as"—she looked down and read off the sheet—"'Always willing to stand up for others.' 'Always has something nice to say.'"

I shrugged. "I mean, I am the head of the yearbook committee, so you can probably do the math."

She glared at me. "You did this because it was the only way you could ever win anything. You couldn't even win a stupid, pointless spelling bee *no one* cared about."

I moved my eyes back down to my poll and picked up my pencil, trying to act casual even though my fingers trembled a little. "You know, Valerie"—my heart pounded, and my cheeks blazed—"I don't think I'll put you down for kindest classmate."

"And still, despite your best efforts, I bet you won't win anything," Emma added.

I dropped my pencil and looked up at her. "Emma."

She stared right back at me. "Yes, loser?"

None of this could be fixed overnight. Amelioration takes time. A-M-E-L-I-O-R-A-T-I-O-N. Amelioration.

But I had to believe that just as being quiet had gotten easier over time, speaking out would get easier, too. I just needed a lot more practice, and here was my chance to get some. Even though my heart still pounded and my cheeks still burned and my hands still shook (which I hid), I stared Emma right in the eyes and told her, "Go fry an asparagus."

chapter 43

Catharsis.
C-A-T-H-A-R-S-I-S.
Catharsis.

Mom, Dad, and I stood outside my bedroom window, all three of us staring at it, analyzing it. The air was clear again, and Mom and Dad were pretty much convinced all the dust storms were over. I knew without a doubt that they wouldn't be coming back. That *he* wouldn't be coming back. And again, I wondered for the millionth time about him.

"Do we really need to do this?" Mom asked.

"We're not doing anything," said Dad. "Avalyn is doing all the . . . doing."

Mom turned her head to me. "Do you really need

to do this? The window guy said we could run a utility knife around the edge and take it out carefully without breaking it."

Dad rolled his eyes at her. "I have literally told you ten times. It's tempered glass, which is literally safety glass."

Mom glared at him. "I literally don't think you could use that word more."

"I literally could," said Dad. "Anyway, this is quicker than the utility knife method."

"I don't know," Mom grumbled.

Dad gripped her by the shoulders. "She could literally jump through the glass and be okay."

My eyes widened. "Really?" I asked excitedly.

Dad released Mom and pointed at me. "Don't even think about it. That's where I draw the line."

"It's going to make such a mess." Mom narrowed her eyes at Dad. "Are you going to be the one to clean it up?"

"Yes, I will." He gazed down at me. "Avalyn needs this. I don't know why. But she does."

I ran my hand over the rough, etched glass. "Destructive therapy," I reminded them. I'd looked it up, built my case, and talked them into it. "Catharsis. C-A-T-H-A-R-S-I-S. Catharsis."

"Right," said Dad. "Destructive therapy."

Mom sighed. "Well, it will certainly be destructive."

Dad gave Mom a warm, understanding look. "It's time to let go a little. Don't you think?"

Mom smirked. "You mean let her spread her wings and fly?"

I snorted while I slipped on my gloves, and Dad smiled. "That's exactly what I mean. We can't be there to protect her every second of her life. And... I think she's shown us she's capable of making good choices. We have to trust her."

Mom gazed at me for a second. Then she picked up the hammer and placed it in my gloved hands. "I do trust her."

"Ready, then?" said Dad, and the three of us put on our goggles.

"Ready," I said.

Dad took a couple of steps back. "It might take a few whacks."

"I'll give it as many as I have to."

Then Mom joined Dad, while I faced the etched glass and swung the hammer.

chapter 44

Doughtiness.
D-O-U-G-H-T-I-N-E-S-S.
Doughtiness.

Nan ran across the cool decking in her purple bikini.

"I'm a teenager!" she screamed, leaping into the blue sparkling water of her new pool.

She had insisted on being the first one to get to feel the water, and we'd all agreed because it was her birthday after all, and her pool. As soon as she hit the water, though, Dillon and I jumped in, too. And then the rest of the party joined us. Nan had pretty much invited everyone in our class, and a bunch of people actually came. It was like a whole new beginning.

Some people think water is a great conductor—

that that's why you're not supposed to swim during thunderstorms. But the truth is, pure water is a terrible conductor; it doesn't conduct electricity at all. But you never find completely pure water in nature. It's all the stuff that's in the water that conducts—the minerals, salt, chemicals, sunblock, and probably some pee.

Floating in that cool clear pool on that warm clear day, I felt so many feelings—excitement, joy, nervousness, exhilaration—all multiplied by the number of bodies in the pool. I felt only good intentions. And hope. There was a lot of hope floating in that pool.

"I can't wait for the school year to be over," Nan said over the splashing and laughing. "This is what we'll be doing every day."

"No more hose fights," I said.

"No, just splash fights." Dillon slammed his hand into the water and showered my face. I put my hands on his shoulders and jumped up, pushing him under the water for a split second before he burst back up and splashed me again.

After about an hour of pool time, Nan's mom called us out for pizza. I toweled off and walked over and asked, "Which is mine?"

Nan's mom smiled at me. "You can pick from whichever one you like, Avalyn."

Nan's mom knew better than anyone I couldn't have regular pizza. Was she having some kind of brain fart? "But which one is gluten and dairy free?" I asked.

"They all are, sweetie." She patted my wet head.

"Today we're *all* eating tofu cheese and cauliflower crust, Avalyn," Nan said, dripping water all over the cool decking.

I gazed over the half dozen pizzas with all different toppings—pepperoni, sausage, veggie, plain cheese. Well, tofu cheese. "You guys didn't have to do that," I murmured.

"We know," said Nan's mom. "But everyone should have at least one day when they get to feel totally included. It was Nan's idea."

I smiled at my best friend, and she said, "Yeah, you can eat the cake, too."

Dillon already had a slice of pepperoni in his hand, his mouth stuffed full of pizza. "And this pizza isn't even disgusting. It's pretty good, actually."

As everyone lined up for pizza, it really did feel nice to be able to pick whatever I wanted. I couldn't remember that ever happening before, except at home. I knew I'd never forget this day.

The three of us sat down together with our pizza and sodas at the patio table. Suddenly, Dillon's mouth dropped open, his slice midway to his mouth, drooping in his hand.

"What?" I turned to see what he was looking at.

Caleb stood in front of us, a small wrapped gift held in his hands, the party going almost totally silent. "I rang the doorbell, but no one answered." He shifted from foot to foot in his flip-flops.

I glanced at Nan, but she looked as surprised as the rest of us.

Nan's mom took the small gift from Caleb's hands. "Nice of you to come." Then she carried it to the folding table piled with the rest of the gifts.

Caleb stood there in his swim shorts and T-shirt, rubbing his neck, his eyes darting around the yard like they didn't know what to land on. The rest of the party went back to pizza and swimming, but the three of us sat quietly, our food untouched.

"It's a necklace," Caleb blurted out. "The gift, I mean. A purple heart necklace." His face was beet red, and I wasn't sure whether it was from the heat or something else. "You seem to like purple."

Nan looked at me with wide eyes, and I shrugged a tiny bit. Then she turned back to Caleb. "Thanks for coming," she said.

Dillon's face was wary. "We're kind of surprised you did."

Caleb tentatively moved closer. It was weird to see him looking so out of place. Without the Meanie Butt Band around him, for once he didn't have the upper hand.

"I just want to say..." Caleb breathed in deeply, squeezing his hands together. Hands that had kept my inhaler from me. Hands that had made mean gestures at all of us. Hands that had written nasty words on papers and chalkboards. "I'm sorry," he finally managed to get out. "I'm sorry for everything."

"You're sorry *today*," said Dillon. "What about when the rest of your friends are around?"

Caleb looked down at his flip-flops. Rubbed his bare arms. "I don't really have any friends. I don't... I don't know what they are."

The three of us looked at one another, trying to

decide what to do. How to respond. Whether to forgive. Whether to trust. Honestly, I felt bad for Caleb
that he didn't even know what it meant to have real
friends—friends who didn't pressure you into doing
things you didn't want to do. Friends who liked you
even when you were different or weird or not like anyone else.

I pushed the fourth chair out with my bare foot.
"You want to sit with us?"

Caleb's head shot up, and he smiled. "Yeah."

When he sat down, I let his foot brush mine. In
that small touch, I felt all the things I'd felt in the
pool. But mostly, there was that hope for a new beginning. And deep, deep down inside, I felt something
else from Caleb. He'd just been waiting for someone
to let him know that he didn't have to do what he'd
been doing. He didn't have to follow the others and
do what they told him. He didn't have to be a bully.

Then I looked around at everyone else at Nan's
party. A lot of them had been like Caleb—just going
along with everything. But things had been changing since the spelling bee. Something was different.

Because it turns out pain isn't the only thing that
spreads like dust in a dust storm. Bravery is like that,

too. Courage. Doughtiness. D-O-U-G-H-T-I-N-E-S-S. Doughtiness.

A lot of kids had been waiting for someone to let them know that they could speak out. That they could say stop. That they could fight back. That things didn't have to stay the way they'd always been.

I guess some people just needed it spelled out for them first.

Epilogue.
E-P-I-L-O-G-U-E.
Epilogue.

One Year Later

It was strangely quiet and empty when I walked into my house, but then I noticed the *Congrats* balloons in the corner and the streamers over the kitchen table. Then I heard a snort coming from behind the couch.

"All right, what's happening?" I said to the not-so-empty room.

Dillon and Nan appeared from behind the couch, and Mom and Dad jumped out of the kitchen. "Surprise!" they all yelled, not even remotely in unison.

"What's this?"

Dad lifted the cake in his hands. "Surprise congratulations party."

I read the frosting letters. "'Congrats, Spelling Bee Champ.'"

"Like we said"—Dad grinned—"congrats." Then he opened his mouth wide and made a weird blowing-out-breath sound.

I laughed. "What are you doing?"

"Cheering-crowd noises."

I looked back down at the cake with its bright yellow bees flying around the letters. "But how'd you get this made on such short notice?"

Dad scoffed. "Are you kidding? We ordered it last week."

Mom put an arm around me. "We had no doubts."

"But what if I'd lost?" The cake would've been kind of depressing if that had been the case.

"We had one on backup." He put a hand to his chest and made a sad face. "Sorry for your loss."

Mom slapped his arm. "There was no backup cake."

I laughed and sat down at the table with Nan and Dillon while Dad dished out slices of cake and Mom scooped coconut-milk ice cream. "So what's next?" asked Dillon.

"The district spelling bee," I said. "And then county and regional."

I knew I'd go to them all. I *rarely* misspelled.

It had been a year since I bombed the spelling bee. Since I fought back the giant wall of dust. A year since I last saw Adam. I'd thought about him a lot since then. After Adam left Clear Canyon City, I had constantly watched the weather channel, tracking the dust storms all around the desert. There were a lot of dust storms around Florence for a few months. I did an online search and found a boys' foster group home there. I called them, but they couldn't tell me anything. Privacy laws or something like that.

Then the storms in Florence suddenly stopped and there seemed to be an uptick around Casa Grande, but not so frequently. And not so severe. Then those stopped, too. Of course, there was still the odd dust storm around the valley after that, but they seemed to be random. Nothing I could track. No patterns. No way of knowing where he might be. I didn't know what that meant.

"Oh, Avalyn." Mom picked up something from the kitchen counter. "This came in the mail for you today."

I stared at the large yellow envelope in her hands. "Who's it from?"

Mom shrugged. "No return address. But it looks like it was mailed out of Buckeye." She set the envelope down on the table in front of me and pointed at the postmark with its date and location stamped in red ink.

I ran my finger around the edge of the envelope before ripping the top open. I turned it over and a stack of photographs fell onto the table. Everyone gathered around to see.

The first picture was of a saguaro in bloom. I looked on the back, but nothing was written on it. The second picture was of a couple of kids feeding chickens. The kids in the picture didn't seem to realize someone was taking pictures of them. Again, I studied the back for clues, but the only words were the brand of paper that was used to print the pictures.

Some goats were in the next picture. A farm? I studied the photos one by one—an older man playing catch with a little boy in a big grassy yard. An older woman with short silver hair laughing in a kitchen with a toddler on her hip. Her grandchild? Three young kids sitting in a tree and making silly faces. And then a simple house with grass and trees around it. But in the distance, I could make out the mountains of the west side of the valley—Buckeye. Where the envelope had come from.

My heart sped up as I realized these pictures were telling me a story. A very important story.

A story just for me.

"That's odd," said Dad. "Who do you think sent those?"

I swallowed and gathered the pictures and envelope into a stack. "I don't know," I said. "I'm just going to put them away." I left the table and went to my room, gently shutting the door.

I sat down on my bed and laid the pictures out one by one, studying them. The last picture in the stack was of the house in Buckeye again, this time with a large group of people standing in front of it— the older man and woman and all the children from the other pictures. I counted them—fourteen children of all shades and shapes and ages and colors. No, not fourteen. *Fifteen.* The fifteenth was behind the camera, taking the picture.

I looked in the envelope again and realized a photo was still stuck inside. I pulled it out.

It was a picture of me.

The picture was taken from a distance. It was of me sitting at a table in a dark, quiet corner. Me in the Target dress I'd bought with Nan. Me smiling a nervous smile. Nervous to be at the dance.

I looked at the picture a long time, remembering that night. Remembering that girl. She was very different from who I was now. What I went through after that night changed me. I'd like to think I was stronger than the girl in the picture. Braver than she was, too, though she did knock a bowl of dirt out of Bryden's hand. I smiled at the memory.

I slowly turned the picture over and finally found words scrawled on the back. Just two of them.

Thank you.

That was all. But it was enough. Because these pictures and those two words answered all the questions I'd had over the last year.

My eyes burned, and I swallowed down the thickness in my throat while I looked over the pictures again. And again. Then I placed them carefully in my dresser drawer, making sure not to bend or wrinkle them, and closed it gently.

I picked up the empty sea glass frame and opened the back. I'd kept one picture out, the one of the saguaro in bloom, and I slipped it inside the frame. Then I placed it back on my dresser and stared at it—a reminder that even after the worst drought and dust storms, something could still survive. And not just survive, but bloom bigger and more beautiful than ever before.

I sat on my bed and gazed at the clear blue sky, through the new window Mom and Dad had installed. My friends and parents laughed about something in the other room. I hadn't used my rescue inhaler a single time this week, so I pushed my window open and breathed in the fresh desert air, listening to the absolute stillness, only interrupted by the odd call of a cactus wren and the soft murmur of voices in the kitchen. A pair of quail walked by, pecking at the ground. One of them stopped and made a squeaking sound. Three tiny babies burst out from under a nearby bush to catch up to them.

Of course, there would always be dust storms. They couldn't stay away forever. But today, from Clear Canyon City all the way to Buckeye, the skies were clear and calm and quiet.

Author's Note

A lot of children, far too many children, have been hurt or are currently being hurt by someone in their life. In this story, Adam was being hurt by his uncle. You may be wondering why Adam didn't report it. Why he didn't fight back. Adam didn't tell on his abuser for a lot of the same reasons that many children don't tell on the people hurting them. It's because he was scared. Because he was confused about what was happening to him. He was ashamed and even wondered if what was happening to him was somehow his fault. Abusers are good at making children believe it's their fault, even though it never is. Adam was afraid he would get in trouble if people found out. He didn't know where he would go if he couldn't stay with his uncle anymore.

As a mom of three daughters, I've tried to protect my girls by talking to them about these things from a very young age. I believe that something that could've protected Adam is simply knowing. Knowing that what his uncle was doing to him is evil and a serious crime. Knowing that he could report it and not get in trouble. Knowing that it was never his fault. Knowing that there are people who can help stop it from happening again.

Someone may be hurting you, but you're scared to tell on them.

Tell anyway.

Maybe the person hurting you has told you to keep what they're doing to you a secret or has even threatened you if you tell.

Tell anyway.

Maybe you're worried you'll get in trouble if you tell. Maybe the person hurting you has convinced you it's your fault.

Tell anyway. It's not your fault.

Maybe the person hurting you is someone you love. Someone you're supposed to be able to trust. Someone who's supposed to take care of you and protect you. I'm so, so sorry.

Tell anyway.

Who should you tell? Tell someone you trust who hasn't hurt you. That could be a parent, grandparent, aunt, or other family member. It could be someone at school—a counselor, teacher, coach, or librarian. In the story, Avalyn tells the school nurse that she believes Adam is being abused by his uncle.

If you tell someone and nothing happens, then tell someone else. And then tell another person. Keep telling until you find someone who believes and supports you.

Have you ever heard the saying that knowledge is power? Now you know. You can speak out. You can say stop. You can fight back. And the best way to fight back against your abuser is to tell. In the words of Avalyn's dad: It's not even a choice. You *have* to tell.

If someone is hurting you, you can call 1-800-4-A-CHILD or visit their website at www.childhelp .org.

For more information on this most important subject, I recommend the following books: *What Does Consent Really Mean* by Pete and Thalia Wallis, *Consent (for Kids!): Boundaries, Respect, and Being in Charge of YOU* by Rachel Brian, and *Please Tell: A Child's Story About Sexual Abuse* by Jessie.

For children recovering from abuse, I recommend *The PTSD Survival Guide for Teens* by Sheela

Raja and Jaya Raja Ashrafi, *Healing Days: A Guide for Kids Who Have Experienced Trauma* by Susan Farber Straus, and *How Long Does It Hurt?: A Guide to Recovering from Incest and Sexual Abuse for Teenagers, Their Friends, and Their Families* by Cynthia L. Mather.

For further middle-grade reading, I recommend *Fighting Words* by Kimberly Brubaker Bradley and *When You Know What I Know* by Sonja K. Solter.

Discussion Questions

1. Avalyn calls the bullies at her school the Meanie Butt Band. How can giving something a name empower you?

2. Why does Avalyn want to be a spelling bee champion?

3. Avalyn admits to Adam (and herself) that she doesn't have a lot in common with her best friends, Dillon and Nan, beyond one very important thing: "We just really like each other" (p. 43). How can mutual like and respect be a foundation for friendship even without shared interests?

4. Avalyn's school has a zero-tolerance policy for bullying, yet bullying still happens. How? Have you witnessed bullying at your school? What can kids *actually* do about it?

5. Why does Dillon want to go to the school dance? Why doesn't Avalyn or Nan?

6. Even though Adam is a new friend, Avalyn can sense that something's wrong, and she finds the courage to tell him so (p. 186). How is voicing her concern an act of courage?

7. Why do you think Avalyn struggles to speak up when Bryden, Caleb, Valerie, and Emma bully and assault her and her friends? When Dillon angrily tells Avalyn, "You didn't say *anything*," she thinks to herself, "My silence said *everything*" (p. 232). What does she mean?

8. What does Avalyn believe is causing the dust?

9. What does Avalyn discover about Adam? Talk with a grown-up about how that revelation makes you feel.

10. Avalyn's dad tells her, "If you know someone is being hurt, then no matter what your friend

wants—even if you think they won't want to be friends with you anymore—no matter what may happen...you *have* to tell" (p. 266). How is he right?

11. How was Caleb showing up at Nan's pool party an act of courage? How was Avalyn's welcoming of him one, too?

12. Avalyn says that her superpower would be spelling. Do you think she has other powers? What would your superpower be?

13. Avalyn's parents tell her that what she does with her breath can change the world (Prologue). How does she end up using her breath to create change? What would you like to do with your breaths?

Acknowledgments

Thank you so much to all the people who worked so hard to make this book what it is. Thank you especially to my editor, Lisa Yoskowitz, whose wisdom and advice always make my books so much better than they would've been. Thank you also to Caitlyn Averett and Lily Choi for their valuable contributions. Thank you to Karina Granda and Yaoyao Ma Van As for creating a cover more beautiful than anything I could have imagined. And thank you to everyone else at Little, Brown Books for Young Readers who continues to support me and my stories.

Thank you to my literary agent, Shannon Hassan, for the constant support and feedback. Thank you to my best friends, Kelly deVos, Stephanie Elliot, and Lorri Phillips, who are always there to listen and laugh. Thank you to my husband and three daughters, who give my life meaning and purpose. Thank you, God, for putting all these people in my life.

I am so grateful to the many librarians, educators, booksellers, and book reviewers who continue to recommend my books to readers. Your enthusiasm allows me to keep doing the job I love. But most of all, thank you to my young readers. Keep reading and I'll keep writing.

Sheli Walters

DUSTI BOWLING

is the bestselling and award-winning author of *Insignificant Events in the Life of a Cactus, Momentous Events in the Life of a Cactus, 24 Hours in Nowhere,* the Aven Green chapter book series, *The Canyon's Edge,* and *Across the Desert.*

Dusti's books have won the Reading the West Book Award, the Sakura Medal, a Golden Kite Honor, and the William Allen White Children's Book Award. They have been nominated for over thirty state awards. Her books are Junior Library Guild selections and have been named best books of the year by the Chicago Public Library, *Kirkus,* Bank Street College of Education, A Mighty Girl, Shelf Awareness, and many more.

Dusti holds degrees in psychology and education and lives in Arizona with her husband, three daughters, and a bunch of farm animals.